PAWNS
in the
GAME

Daniel Montvydas

NEWMAN SPRINGS PUBLISHING
320 Broad Street
Red Bank, NJ 07701

First originally published by Newman Springs Publishing 2022

Reader discretion is advised. This is a work of fiction.
All characters, places, persons, and things you see in this
novel are fictitious; and any connections to real persons,
places, or things are completely coincidental.

ISBN 978-1-68498-513-5 (Paperback)
ISBN 978-1-68498-514-2 (Digital)

Printed in the United States of America

To Thomas "Fish" Bowdren; Mr. Patragnoni; Mr. Coyle; my parents, David and Nicole; my siblings, Tom, Liv, Soph, Joey, Becca, and Max; and all my friends, additional family, and anyone who inspired a character in my book.

Prologue

A man is standing over his living room table, staring at a mirror in overwhelming despondency. He stares at the mirror and mumbles to himself for a few fleeting seconds before slamming his fist on the table, grabbing his jacket and traversing out of his cold, barren Philadelphian apartment.

He heaves himself down the street, kicking up the rocks that litter the minor road in his tracks, the early morning sun glaring off his paper-thin glasses. He reaches into his jacket, covered in sewn-on patches, and pulls out a pack of cigarettes. He peers inside the pack, his eyes revealing only two cigarettes remaining.

"Damn it."

He sighs angrily and sticks one of his remaining cigarettes into his mouth, pulling out a match to light it. He watches the flame burn the paper ever so slightly and shakes the match out, avoiding any minor burns on his fingertips. He takes a light drag from it and continues rolling down the street toward the neighborhood coffee shop. As he enters, the barista seems somewhat annoyed by his presence in the shop. He walks up to the counter and speaks in a shy voice, his Irish accent piercing through the air like the smell of whiskey off a drunk.

"Black coffee. That's all."

"Buck twenty."

He reaches into his pocket and pulls out a dollar bill and a nickel. He sticks the cigarette into his mouth and holds his finger up, searching his pockets to scrounge up any spare change. After searching his seemingly endless amount of jacket pockets, he pulls out a dime and two pennies.

"Buck seventeen's all I got."

The barista picks up the money and throws it angrily into the register with a kind of annoyance that embarrasses him as he blushes and gulps down empty air.

"I want my three cents tomorrow morning."

The man nods somberly as he waits silently at the counter, watching the barista fill up a cup with coffee and hands it to him. He kindly thanks the barista for their generosity and rolls over to a small table in a lonely corner of the shop.

He smokes and drinks and smokes and drinks. He shakes his cup and pops the lid open, seeing a small amount of coffee remaining at the bottom. He peers around the shop conspiratorially, looking to see if anyone is watching him. Seeing no one, he reaches into his patchy jacket pocket and pulls out a stainless steel flask and pours out whiskey into his cup, pulling it away after a few seconds. He puts the lid back on the cup and takes a sip, feeling the burn of the whiskey and the bitterness of the coffee engulf in his mouth and in his stomach. He finishes the cup, throws it out, and leaves the shop, heading back to his lonely apartment after calming his nerves. As he's walking down the street, he suddenly and fearfully feels his hairs stick up on the back of his neck.

He watches slowly as a glossy black Cadillac rolls by him quickly but slows down as it approaches a man about one hundred feet in front of him, dressed head to toe in an all-brown suit with a matching hat to boot. He watches in eloquent horror as the windows roll down slowly and a singular revolver is stuck out the windowless vacancy, firing what seems to be an endless number of shots, as they echo down the busy street and ring throughout his head like a bad dream.

After around ten seconds, the gun disappears back into the unknown vehicle, and it races down the street at an illicit speed. The man, after dropping to the ground in fear, stands up and begins slowly walking over to the man, lifelessly spread-eagle on the sidewalk, blood spilling out of him down the sidewalk over the curb and down a storm drain about ten feet away like a calm river of death.

He didn't know it then, but the man had been a witness to a mob killing by a ruthless hitman, a wise guy so notorious and murderous that if even so much as made a bad joke with his name in it, you'd be dead by sundown. That man was none other than Donald McCullough, or better known as Donnie Just.

I

Six-Month-Old
Philadelphian Home

Ever since he was a teenager, Donnie McCullough has been surrounded by the lifestyle of men who come home with rolls and rolls
of hundred-dollar bills while he watched his father come home to
his lowly wife, his mother, crushed under the pressure of a hard
day's work with little pay. He watched him come home like that for
ten years. He would come home to three young children, but since
Donnie was the oldest, he was always entrusted as the babysitter to
his younger siblings as well as the designated punching bag.

Donald Aingeal McCullough was born on March 25, 1949, in
Cork County, Ireland. His mother is a seamstress, and his father works
at a whiskey distillery. Donnie quickly learns that he isn't wanted in
his family. Once Donnie can comprehend what his parents are saying, he learns that he is an accidental pregnancy. His father doesn't
want him, but his mother insists. And on that fateful day in March
1949, Donnie comes into this world, loved by one parent and hated
by the other.

As Donnie grows and builds his body up, his father begins to
beat him. Regularly, his father comes home, ragged and dirty, and he
would beat the living hell out of Donnie. But no matter how hard
Donnie is beaten or how hard his mother cries and tells his father to

stop, he never dares to put a hand on her. He would beat Donnie two to three times a week, sometimes digging his steel-toed boots into his ribcage as Donnie lies on his bedroom floor crying. He always tells him to stop. He never does.

At some point, Donnie becomes accustomed to the abuse, as a dog becomes accustomed to treats. It happens to Donnie every night now. Like clockwork. Regardless, Donnie would accept the beatings. He takes it like a man. He swears that it helps him grow, that this abusive shell of a man is making him who he is today and by God, he hates his guts for it.

Once his mother has Ronan, Donnie's baby brother, he begins beating him too when he becomes of age. Donnie is around seven years old when his father starts beating his baby brother, who is around five. He wants to stop him, but he didn't have the guts to stop his father. He beats his baby brother endlessly, even worse than him and more consistently than him, but no matter how hard his mother hits him back and tells him to stop, he never dares to lay a hand on her.

The McCulloughs move to America two years later after Donald's father gets laid off from his distillery job. They hop on a boat and land in the port of Philadelphia by early spring of 1959, and by December of that year, his mother gives birth to their one and only girl, Finley McCullough.

When his father finds out his mother gave birth to a girl, he is livid. He had always talked about wanting only boys as his children, but Donnie and Ronan know he only wants a new punching bag. He is getting tired of Donnie and Ronan who are about ten and eight years old respectively by the time Finley comes into the picture. Regardless, their old man continues his beatings.

With his new job as a union man working as a longshoreman, his anger and his drunkenness heightens, making him become stone-cold and ruthless; but no matter what or how he feels, he never dares to lay a hand on their mother.

He would come home some nights; and Donnie's mother would scream bloody murder at their father, telling him he doesn't make enough money for this, that, or the other thing and boy, oh boy, his old man would scream back. So loud, everyone in a three-block radius would have called the cops before he finished his screaming fit.

He'd get all in his mother's face, so close that she could feel the heat off his drunken breath and the spittle erupt from his mouth onto her cheeks. He would raise his hands, coming within inches of her face to point, scream and shout at her; but he never dares lay a hand on her. Donnie would lie on his bed, his face under his pillow, crying as his brother hides under his bed in fear.

They know that once he is done, he would come for one of them. Which one, they never knew. Often, it is the first one he spots, but on days like these, they'd never know. Sometimes, it feels like a game with him: which kid could take the beating, which kid could last longer, which kid could take it like a man. One dreadful night goes too far, and things take a turn for the worst.

After his spiel at their mother, Donnie's father storms into Donnie and Ronan's room, and Donnie peeks his eyes out from under his covers just as he storms into their room like a raging bull. He wants to hide his face, but he can't. As his father comes in, Donnie locks eyes with him immediately, and in that moment, he knows his father would pick him.

Instead, he snarls loudly, something he had never seen before. He stomps over to Ronan's bed and reaches under it quickly, harshly dragging Ronan across the bedroom floor before lifting him in the air with one hand, Ronan's frail eight-year-old body flailing aimlessly while he cries hysterically with fear. His father looks at Donnie with a look that shakes him to his core. He had always only used his body to hit them: his hands, his boots, his elbows, or his knees. The only item he would regularly use to beat us is his brown hard-leather belt, cracked all over its body to add extra sting whenever it connected with human skin.

This time is different.

This time, he reaches into their closet and grabs Ronan's baseball bat. Before leaving the room, his father smiles at Donnie, as if this is a test. Their house is two stories tall, with a basement under the first floor. Donnie and Ronan's room, along with their parents' room, is on the second floor. Their bathroom, living room, dining room, and kitchen are all on the first floor.

His baby brother, screaming mercilessly at the top of his lungs, is taken downstairs into the basement. Donnie listens in horror as his brother's screams fade from the echoes of his room to the basement. Even with the two floors separating them, Donnie still hears Ronan's terrified cries of help. Finley is around five or six months old and had woken up during his parents' fight, crying her baby cry, causing his mother to break into tears as she picks her up, trying to calm her down.

As he hears the basement door shut, he knows what the old man is doing to him. He is testing him. He wants to see if Donnie is man enough to save his baby brother. He has been so scared until that point. Then, something inside Donnie snaps. He opens his closet and grabs his own baseball bat. As he walks to the stairs, he sees his baby sister Finley, crying so loudly, it is driving his mother insane.

He sees his mother in his father's dresser, poking and prodding around, looking for something. He doesn't know what it is, and he doesn't care. He storms down the steps, past the living room and into the dining room, which leads to the top of the basement steps. He storms down the basement steps, just as his father is about to raise the bat to hit his brother as he lets out a scream.

"HEY!"

His father whips around quickly, his eyes meeting the sight of Donnie's four foot four, seventy-five-pound frame, wielding a baseball bat about half his size, his face full of anger and pain. His father lets out a quick audible laugh before Donnie screams at him, his voice cracking with anger.

"Don't you fuckin' touch him again!"

Donnie quickly cut his father's laugh off. Donnie sees that his father doesn't like that he had cursed at him. That is the first time Donnie has ever cursed, let alone at his own father. His father drops the bat and comes steaming toward Donnie as quick as his old man body can. After years of beating, he knows his style by heart.

Donnie ducks under his father as he reaches to grab Donnie's shirt; and he smacks him square in the shins with the meat of the bat, causing his father to fall face first, breaking his nose on the hard, concrete floor. His father gets back on his hands and knees as blood pours unceasingly out of his nose. This is the first time Donnie has seen his old man bleed.

Donnie doesn't know what to do after that. He freezes, and before he knows it, his father reaches around Donnie and grabs the baseball bat from his hands. But instead of beating Donnie, his father presses the thin grip of the bat over Donnie's throat, slowly crushing it. Luckily, Donnie pushes away just enough to prevent that from happening, but he can't last long. His father is still his old man and a lot stronger than Donnie is.

Relentlessly, his father presses against Donnie's throat, his body slowly becoming more and more sluggish and heavy as his arms become tired from holding back the bat. He hears a pounding in his ears, and he isn't sure if it is his brother running up the basement steps to safety or the blood pounding in his brain. Donnie can't believe it. His old man is about to kill him.

Then suddenly, poof! The grip loosens entirely, and he inhales so quickly, Donnie feels his brain thank his lungs for breathing again. He wonders why everything stopped so suddenly, and he looks over his shoulder and sees a look on his father's face that he had never seen before.

Fear.

Donnie crawls away from his old man, who has his hands sticking up with his elbows at a ninety-degree angle, like a scared human pitchfork. He looks over and sees Ronan, his face stained with remnants of tears but silent, staring at something. He isn't staring at his father but something behind him. Donnie backs away from his father and stands up quickly, trying to gain some composure as his body is still recovering from his near-death experience.

As Donnie backs away, his eyes widen with shock as he sees his mother, holding a revolver to the back of his father's head. Donnie can tell his mother is struggling to keep it upright, but she holds the gun well, digging the tip of the muzzle into the nape of his old man's head. Her face is saddened but also emboldened as she speaks in a calm, soothing manner.

"Ronan, Donald, go up the steps and run out of the house. Don't stop. Run to Jamey's house. I'll pick you up soon. I love you both."

Even though she speaks with motherly love, her voice cracks with pain, her face resisting the urge of more tears. Donnie walks over to Ronan and picks him up, walking up the stairs. He never takes his eyes off his mother until he makes it into the living room. Once Donnie and Ronan get into the living room, they run out of the house as fast as they can. Ronan cries, and Donnie tells him to shut up and keep running. After running for a block, they hear a loud bang come from their house.

Ronan screams through his tears, "What the hell was that?"

Donnie screams back, "Shut the fuck up and keep running!"

They run for what seems like forever, finally getting to his friend Jamey Giambruno's house. Jamey opens the door to the ghastly sight of Donnie and Ronan, both with bruises and looks of pain and sadness covering their faces. Jamey lets them immediately; and his mother, Mrs. G, comes into the room, looking at our faces with a look of extreme concern.

"Oh my Lord, what happened?!"

Ronan is crying so hard, he can't form a complete sentence without breaking down even more. Donnie tells Jamey to take Ronan into the kitchen to give him some ice for his wounds as Donnie explains to Mrs. G what had happened. Donnie explains the whole thing, Mrs. G not interrupting Donnie for anything. She just sits there, listening to what he has to say, and in that very moment, that is all Donnie needs. Donnie just wants someone to listen to him, to listen to his pain. Up to that point, no one had known that their father had beaten Donnie or Ronan.

After he finishes his story, Mrs. G stands up and gives Donnie a big hug, and before that moment, Donnie hadn't shed a tear. He was too angry. But as Mrs. G hugs Donnie, he cries waterfalls. After her warm, motherly embrace, she walks over to the phone and picks it up off the receiver.

"Donnie, you know I have to call the police, right?"

Now, even with everything his father had done, after years and years of beatings to him and Ronan, Donnie doesn't want him to go to jail. As much as he hates his old man's guts, he doesn't want Finley to grow up without a father. Regardless, through teary eyes, Donnie nods at Mrs. G as she dials those three dreaded numbers. Hordes of blue boys fly past the Giambruno household and down the block, stopping in front of Donnie's six-month-old Philadelphian home.

About a half hour after leaving the house, Donnie is sitting in the living room, staring at the floor. He turns around to the sound of Jamey walking down the steps from the second floor of his house.

"Ronan was in pain, but he also looked exhausted. He laid him down on my bed and fell asleep in an instant."

Jamey is the best. Donnie had met Jamey from around the neighborhood, and they became friends instantly. They played baseball, basketball, football, soccer—anything physical—including fighting the neighborhood kids they didn't like. Jamey, even though Donnie is his best friend, grew fond of Ronan quickly, and they'd often invite him out to play with them.

Jamey always loved Ronan.

Jamey walks over to Donnie and sits down next to him. Jamey knows Donnie wants to talk to someone, but he also knows that Donnie needs time to think, to process the horrific experience that he had just been through. Jamey pats Donnie's back somberly as he reaches for the TV remote, knowing that some TV show would help take their minds off everything that had happened.

As they are skipping through the television channels, they cruise past the nightly news; and like a bullet, Donnie places his hand on Jamey's finger, which is consistently pressing the Up button on the remote. Donnie nods at him once, and Jamey knows exactly what he wants him to do. He presses the Down button twice, and there it is, right there on the news channel: Donnie's six-month-old Philadelphian home, glued to the television for the entire city to see.

II

Part of the Family

The newsperson reporting the story talks in such a fake way. Even at that age, Donnie wants to reach through the television set and murder him. Donnie watches through Jamey's 1959 TV set as the cops carry his baby sister out of the house. Even through the grain of the news camera, Donnie can see her cry, and even though he is blocks and blocks away, Donnie swears he can even hear it. He watches in horror as the EMTs roll a stretcher out of his home with a body bag zipped up on it. Donnie then watches in soul-crushing sadness as the police escort his father out of his house in handcuffs.

Donnie cracks.

Donnie cries so hard, Jamey doesn't know what to do but to cry with him. Donnie breaks down in Jamey's living room and doesn't stop for what seems like an hour. After he finishes, Donnie just falls asleep in Jamey's living room. Mrs. G doesn't know how long Donnie or Ronan would be there, but she doesn't care. She will care for them for as long as she can. As long as she has to. Mrs. G is happy with how close Donnie is with Jamey and how close Jamey is with him and Ronan. In her eyes, she sees them as her sons, and Jamey sees them as his brothers.

The next day, Donnie wakes up to a knock on the door. Mrs. G is in the kitchen making Donnie, Jamey, and Ronan breakfast, stopping her cooking to open the door. Two cops stand at the door;

and Mrs. G, while not surprised by their presence at her house, is still shocked. Donnie listens intently, trying to figure out what Mrs. G and the cops are talking about.

"Good morning, officers."

"Good morning, Mrs. Giambruno."

Donnie can tell by the way the cop said it that the news he is going to give wasn't good.

"Could you step outside with us for a moment?"

Mrs. G nods once and walks outside of her house, shutting the door behind her. Donnie, pretending to be asleep, immediately shoots up and walks over to the window, hiding behind the curtain to eavesdrop on the conversation.

"We're sorry to inform you of this, Mrs. Giambruno, but Mrs. McCullough was shot and killed yesterday by her husband. Mr. McCullough confessed to everything, including continuous beating of his own sons."

Even though he already saw the news, Donnie still drops to his knees and cries. He had gone to sleep that night, hoping and praying that it was all a bad dream, only to awake on Jamey's living room floor, now knowing for certain it's not. Through uncontrollable tears, he hears the door open and watches Mrs. G and the two cops enter the Giambruno home. Donnie wants to go back under the covers, to pretend he heard nothing, but his body is too overwhelmed with sadness to even move. Mrs. G sees him by the curtains, curled up in a ball, crying hysterically. She gets down on her knees and gives Donnie a hug, as he feels her body convulse slowly, trying to repress her own tears.

After a few seconds, she lets go and Donnie wipes his face. Still on his knees, Donnie looks at the police officers, both standing there silently with hats in their hands. One officer, even with a flourishing 1950s-esque mustache, looks exceptionally young for his look. The officer slowly gets down on one knee and reaches into his pocket, handing Donnie a business card with his name and his personal number on it: Det. Jackson Freeman, Homicide. 555-3247.

"If you ever need anything, call me."

After he hands Donnie his card, Detective Freeman stands up and places his hat back on his head, his partner following suit. Donnie doesn't remember much after that. He remembers the detective and his partner walking Mrs. G out of the house to talk again. It probably has to do with their sister or their father's charges and court case, but probably both. This time, Donnie doesn't listen. He just sits there on Jamey's floor, staring at the detective's card. In that moment, all he knows for sure is that he and Ronan are staying with Mrs. G for the time being.

Donnie loves that woman. Mrs. G treated them like a mother better than Donnie's own did. Donnie loves his own mother, but at times, he hated her. He hated how she never truly tried to stop his old man from beating him or Ronan out of fear of being hit herself. Donnie never hated Mrs. G. She is so kind to him and Ro after everything happened, and once everything gets sorted out, the police come over with Finely who had been with CPS for the last few months.

By the time they welcome Finley into the Giambruno home, she is about a year old, with Ronan being about nine and Donnie about eleven. Since Donnie and Ronan had stayed with Mrs. G for the last few months, CPS asks if Mr. and Mrs. Giambruno would like to be declared legally as guardians of the now orphaned McCullough children. Mrs. G happily agrees, and with Mr. G present, they sign the papers to declare that the McCullough children are now a part of the Giambruno household.

From that point on, life gets easier. Donnie goes out more. He gets to know more of the neighborhood kids. He fights less, and he even begins going to real school. Donnie and Ronan have been homeschooled since they came over to America, but now, Donnie can go to real school as a high schooler. One night, a few weeks into his freshman year, he is up late on a Friday night playing some game with Jamey when he overhears Jamey's parents talking in their bedroom. As Donnie walks up to the door, he must've missed the entire conversation but hears Mrs. G say, "I think it's time now."

She says it with such joy in her voice, and Donnie is confused by what she means until the next morning. It is Donnie, Jamey, Ronan,

Finley, and Mr. and Mrs. G all sitting at the kitchen table, eating their Saturday breakfast and watching TV. While they are eating, they see Mr. G reach for the remote and turn off the TV. He waits silently until all four children are looking at him before speaking. Even before he starts, a smile forms on his rugged Sicilian face. He looks at his wife and his smile widens.

"We got something to tell you kids."

His smile slowly gets bigger and bigger, and knowing it is something good, all four kids' attention is peaked toward Mr. G's voice.

"We talked to CPS and the lawyers, and we got the okay from them. We wanted to let you three kids know that we want to adopt you. Make you truly part of the family. What do ya think?"

Donnie can't believe it. From the moment Mr. G says those words, Donnie can't stop smiling. Neither can Ronan and Finley, though she is young and doesn't fully understand what is happening. But looking at her big brothers, seeing that they are smiling, she smiles too. All they could say through their rapidly rising joy is, "Absolutely!"

Mr. G, Mrs. G, and Jamey shout with joy, with the McCullough trio rising from their seats to give Mr. and Mrs. G enormous hugs. Donnie cries tears of joy, his brother quickly following suit. At last, Donnie is finally a part of something—something that he loves, but more importantly, something that loves him back.

III

Whatta Catchphrase

Now, Donnie Just, or Donnie J, like any other famous wise guy, is known by a variety of aliases and pseudo nicknames. Names to the likes of "Donald Justice," "Don J," "Donnie Just," "Donnie J," or just plain old "Donnie." They derive his nickname from a little catch-phrase he said after whacking a former wise guy.

Donnie is out on a hit with one wise guy he used to hang around a lot. His name was Frankie Garcetti, but everyone calls him Frankie G. Frankie G and Donnie are tasked with whacking a witness in one of Enzo's cases. His name is Jimmy Barseni. Apparently, Jimmy is an undercover fed who had gotten into their wise guy group after being brought in by Frankie G. Frankie G is loved by everyone and hated by no one. But when Enzo found out about Jimmy, the tides had turned in an instant.

Donnie had never worked with Frankie G, but when he first heard about him, it was after they had made Jimmy Barseni out. He and Frankie G are tasked with whacking him, and Donnie is tasked with whacking Frankie G. Donnie had just turned eighteen a month prior, April 25, 1967. On that night, Donnie picks Jimmy up with Frankie G in the passenger seat of his brand-new 1966 Lincoln Continental.

Man, that car is a beaut.

Jimmy is about five foot ten, 180 pounds of lean, Sicilian beef. If they hadn't found out about him, who knows how far he would've gotten up the chain? After picking him up, they drive down Broad Street and stop about a few blocks away from City Hall. They all get out and are about to catch a comedy show by a stand-up comedian by the name of Ricky Packer, who is in Philadelphia for the night. Donnie has no intent of entering the show. All three wise guys are about two blocks from the show place when Frankie G turns into an alley and says, "I know a back way where we can get in for free. I know a guy."

Jimmy doesn't even care. All he says is, "Fine by me. I hate paying for those stupid fuckin' tickets anyways."

Frankie G nods and begins to walk down the alley, with Jimmy right behind him and Donnie pulling up the rear. As Jimmy is about ten feet down the alleyway, All Donnie says is, "Don't worry. After tonight, you won't have to pay for anything."

Jimmy turns around to look at him in confusion, but by the time he faces Donnie, Jimmy's face is met with two clean shots, one hitting the bridge of his nose and the other hitting the upper right section of his forehead. He drops like a wet mop, his head cracking open on the pavement of the alley. The blood splatters backward from the shots, with some getting on Frankie G's suit jacket. He stops as the shots rang out and looks at his jacket, now littered with small specks of blood.

"Oh, you've got to be fuckin' kidding me, Donnie! I just bought this shit. This was fifteen hundred dollars, you thick-headed Irish fuck!"

All Donnie does is walk over to Frankie and tap him on the shoulder.

"Quit your bitching and help me drag him to the side of the alley."

Even though he is pissed, Frankie G grabs Jimmy by the ankles, and Donnie grabs him by his arms. They drag him over to the side of the alley. Donnie looks up at Frankie G, and he is breaking a sweat from pulling Jimmy's corpse. Frankie G isn't no athlete, but he is a big guy, about two hundred pounds squeezed into a five-foot-six frame.

"You need to work out, my portly Italian friend. You seriously broke a sweat pulling him over here?"

Frankie is gassed. He nods at him without speaking a word.

"It was ten fuckin' feet. You're really tired from that?"

Again, Frankie nods at him without speaking a word through his laborious breaths. After a few minutes of catching his breath, Frankie stands up, pulls a handkerchief out of his pocket, dabs his forehead of sweat, and places his handkerchief back into his jacket pocket.

"Okay. I'm hungry. I'm getting Chinese when we get back to the hotel. You want anything?"

Donnie walks up to Frankie G as he is slowly walking out of the alleyway toward the car. Frankie G never saw it coming. Donnie cracks him twice, once behind his left ear and one right in the nape of his neck. He drops like a sack. After he shoots him, Donnie walks away immediately and gets to the car with Maxo Salucci, one of Enzo's capos, waiting inside of it.

Donnie taps on the trunk twice, and Maxo puts the car in reverse and backs into the alleyway. The trunk is lined with disposable plastic wrap and has two large plastic tarps inside of it. He wraps up Jimmy and Frankie G and places them into the trunk of the car. After getting them inside the trunk, Maxo and Donnie are standing over the opened trunk, staring at Frankie G's and Jimmy Barseni's bodies, folded up and crunched into the car trunk like paper towels in a trashcan. Donnie pulls out his signature piece, a chrome-plated .38 snub nose with the Latin word Pacificator etched into the barrel.

Meaning, peacemaker.

Maxo Salucci looks at Donnie, who looks back at him with a calm demeanor.

"Just makin' sure."

He extends his gun-holstered hand and fires two shots into the trunk of the car, one hitting Jimmy in the nose, the other hitting Frankie in the side of his head.

After shutting the trunk, Maxo drives to the Dump, the notorious underworld cemetery of Philadelphia. If you want someone to disappear, you take them to the Dump.

Along with being the driver, Maxo is helping Donnie dump the bodies. In the car's backseat, Maxo has his wide variety of knives and cutting utilities to help easily dispose of the bodies. After getting to the dump, Donnie and Maxo get Frankie G out first since he is bigger and would take more time getting through. He takes about an hour and a half because all his fat and his bones are so goddamn thick.

First, you gotta take off all signs of identification: tattoos, birthmarks, scars, anything.

Cut it off, put it in a bag to burn later.

Then, you cut off the extremities: the feet and the hands, moving up to the arms and legs after. Then, you cut off the head.

For Frankie G, he only has one identification marker, which is a small heart on his left arm that says Mom with an arrow going through the heart. They cut the skin off and place it in a plastic bag, the cheap shit kind you use to carry your groceries in.

After cutting off the head, they start cutting the body up. Before this hit, Donnie had no clue how profitable the human body was, but before they began cutting up Frankie G, Maxo walks back to the car and grabs a large ice cooler. Maxo expertly cuts out the heart, the lungs, the kidneys, the liver, the spleen, and anything else he can. With people like Frankie G, since he is a fat fuck, you'd make some money but not a lot. With people like Jimmy, who is healthy and fit…was healthy and fit, you'd rake in the cash. With all the organs from both guys, Maxo estimates the total price would be around two hundred thousand dollars for both of them.

Donnie is floored. One hundred thousand dollars for a bunch of fuckin' organs. He places them all into individual plastic bags with labels on them, placing them directly into the ice after. After cutting up Frankie G, they place his cut-up body into a large trash bag, with about twenty pounds of weights inside of them. After dumping his body, they move on to Jimmy.

Jimmy is a different story. Though he always wore a suit and you seldom saw them, Jimmy is covered in tattoos: all over his back, his chest, his arms, his legs. Fuck, he even had tats on his ass cheeks. What kinda wise guy has tats on his ass cheek? It is like skinning a goddamn pig. By the time Maxo and Donnie are done with him, Jimmy is practically a skeleton. Maxo gets his organs out, placing them in bags, putting them on ice, and they dump his body too. Maxo looks at his watch, reading 2:35 a.m.

"Yo! It's late. Let's drive by the river to dump the piece, drive by the crematorium to drop off the bags, and get the fuck home."

Donnie looks at himself, butcher's gloves duct-taped at his wrists and an apron covered in the blood of Frankie G and Jimmy Barseni. He takes off the gloves and the apron and places them in Frankie G's bag, with Maxo placing his used items in Jimmy's bag. They drive by the crematorium at around three and drop off the bags for their inside man to cremate. They then drive by the Schuylkill River on their way home around 3:20 a.m. On the way home, Maxo is talking to Donnie about the hits and his particular phrase.

"Now, why'd you shoot them again in the trunk? You cracked them both twice, both of them drop dead. They're more dead than Nat King Cole. Why'd you shoot them again?"

Donnie looks over at Maxo slyly, polishing the chrome top of his piece.

"It's always better to overkill than to underkill. I'd rather be 101 percent sure than 99 percent sure, cause that 1 percent will always bite you in the ass. That's why I always just make sure."

Maxo looks at Donnie, still polishing his gun and nods his head slowly.

"Just makin' sure. Whatta catchphrase."

IV

That's My Boy

It is about high school when everything begins to unravel, where Donnie begins to transfer into his way of life, his life as a wise guy. He is fifteen years old and a sophomore in high school; and his baby brother, Ronan, is a freshman.

Donnie had started getting a job running papers with Jamey for Enzo, his adoptive father. He'd give them a stack of newspapers, anywhere between fifty to one hundred, and Donnie and Jamey would walk around the neighborhood, going door to door and ask people if they wanted to buy the paper.

It was good money.

Donnie and Jamey each get 25 percent of the profits, and Enzo takes the other 50 percent, buying tomorrow's papers that night. They'd sell the papers for ten cents, so after a hundred copies, Donnie and Jamey would have about five bucks each to spend after a day's work. Of course, at fifteen, they didn't have much to spend it on.

Regardless, they'd do their morning routes and then go to school at Our Lady of Ransom High School, an all-boys high school located on the corner of Thompson Street. After school finishes up, instead of going home, they'd go to Mikey's Bar on East Girard Avenue in Fishtown, a small neighborhood in Philadelphia made up of Irish and Polish Americans, but more predominantly the Irish. On the way there, while walking down Thompson, they'd stop at Kline's Italian Market to say hello to Bruno.

Bruno Kline is about sixty years old but had been running that shop since the Prohibition era. He always loved having the neighborhood kids around his shop, offering them candy and free slices of meat, even going as far as to buy food for kids who couldn't afford it. He hated being called Mr. Kline, as it made him sound old, so everyone just called him Bruno. Donnie and Jamey walk up to Bruno, and once they spot him, his face lights up into a smile and they'd make small talk with him.

"Hey Donnie. Hey Jamey."

"Hey Bruno! How've you been? Sandwiches selling well?"

"Yeah. Got a lot of people today. Sold about fifty sandwiches before lunch, and with the lunch rush, I'm about to get some good money for today."

Jamey walks up to the counter where the meats are held and lean on it slightly, peering inside to look at them.

"Got anything fresh today, Bruno?"

Bruno looks at Jamey with a clever smile and walks over to the counter, opening up the back door to grab one of the many logs of various meats.

"Oh boy, do I? Prosciutto di Parma, imported from Italy."

Bruno puts on a small plastic glove and pulls out the large leg-looking meat and places it down on the counter next to the slicer. After taking a quick breather, Bruno picks up the large meat and places it into the slicer, slicing a few pieces off the meat, giving Donnie and Jamey a piece each.

Donnie places the slice of prosciutto into his mouth, and his mouth runs like Niagara Falls as it melts in his mouth. It was the best piece of meat he had ever tasted. Donnie and Jamey just stand there at the counter and savor the slice of meat for what seems like an eternity. If heaven on earth is real, Donnie just placed it in his mouth.

After savoring the slice of meat, Jamey orders a pound to bring home to his mother, and they both leave, waving their goodbyes to Bruno. After stopping out Bruno's, they'd head to Mikey's Bar, wise guy central of Philadelphia.

Now, it was definitely strange to have a Sicilian crime family be run out of an Irish family bar, but after the Don won the bar in a sports bet in '45, the family had been running their business through there ever since. Mikey's Bar, to put it simply, is the recruiting office of the family. Located on the corner of East Girard Avenue, it was home to many men, looking to ease their increasing pains from their daily nine-to-five jobs; but it was heaven for a few men that delightfully called themselves wise guys.

There are guys like Vincenzo "Vinny Ruge" Ruggiero, Salvatore "Sals" Andresano, Tito "Tino" Valentino, and Massimo "Maxo" Salucci—all underbosses who specialized in everything from gambling to running prostitution rings and strip clubs to murder. Then, there are guys like Shane "Books" O'Brien, the bagman for the family, who specializes in loan sharking, shylocking, point-shaving schemes, sports betting, and collecting illicit cash from the family's silent businesses. He is basically the accountant of the family. They ran all of this in the ever-expansive basement of Mikey's Bar.

This place has everything: craps tables, blackjack tables, roulette. Books is even talking about getting a slot machine or two down there to boost revenue. Of course, outside of the gambling areas is a little office where Books and his associates run the point-shaving schemes.

Point-shaving, by all means, is actually quite simple. You bribe a team to not cover a point spread to shave points off the spread. Then, all you do is bet against the bribed team. The easiest and most effective sport to point shave on was basketball because you don't even need to bribe the whole team, just one or two of their key influential players.

Give them a couple hundred bucks, tell them to miss a few shots or turn it over once or twice, and the game was yours. Personally, Donnie hates basketball. He never watched it and doesn't care for it much. Give Donnie a baseball bat or a football, and he'll scream at the TV any day of the week. He just doesn't do that for basketball. but when there's money involved, he doesn't care whether or not he likes it; he wants to make some dough.

Then, there are guys like Nicolo "Nicky Sweeps" Russo, Mickey "Mick" Callghan, Benito "Badger" Balboni, and Salvatore "Sally Two" Banetti who are your run-of-the-mill associates for the family, some of them made men but most working their duties to obtain the title. Regardless of whether you are made or an associate or an underboss or a fuckin' accountant, everyone wears the title of wise guy. These men are available at all hours, day or night, rain, shine, snow, sleet, everything. If their wife is giving birth and they get a phone call from the boss, they'd tell her to hold it in and get to Mikey's because that's what wise guys do. They have each other's backs.

Twenty-four seven, three sixty-five.

After getting to the bar, Donnie and Jamey would sit outside of Mikey's Bar and wait for the wise guys to show up, and they'd park their cars in a lot located a few blocks away. It was crazy. Here, Donnie is, at fifteen years old, not even able to legally drive yet; and he is driving Jaguars, Chryslers, Cadillacs, Buicks, Oldmobiles, and more. Donnie even remembers his first time when he thought he was gonna get arrested.

It is after working at Mikey's for a couple months. He is driving Vinny Ruge's Lincoln Continental, and that car is a beaut. He is driving around the neighborhood when he sees the red and blue in the rearview mirror. He pulls over, and all Donnie is thinking was, Shit. I'm gonna get arrested for the first time.

The officers get out of their car. Donnie's sitting in Vinny's Lincoln, which is pretty much brand spanking new and in pristine condition. The officers walk up to the driver-side window, which is open, and begin conversing with the fifteen-year-old Donnie J.

"Son, do you know how to operate a motor vehicle?"

"Yes, officer, I do."

The officer gives Donnie a disbelieving smirk, adjusting his flashy badge in the process.

"Can I see your license, son?"

"Sorry, officer. I left it in my car."

At this point, the cop is fuming. All Donnie thinks is that if he was the cop dealing with him, he would've knocked himself out. Donnie is being a real asshole, and the cop snaps at him.

"Then whose fuckin' car are you driving, boy?"

Once the officer snaps, Donnie jumps. He almost shits his pants, and he probably would've. But it was Vinny's new car, and he would've killed him if Donnie shit his pants in his new Lincoln. Clenching his cheeks, he responds in a startled tone, "Vinny Ruge's, sir!"

The cop runs, devoid of all emotion. He just stares at Donnie like a blank-faced idiot. He gives his partner a look and nods at him quickly. "Have a nice day, kid."

Donnie doesn't believe it. He is astounded. In that very moment, after Donnie walks back to Mikey's from the lot, Donnie knows he wants to be a wise guy. If you have that type of power over cops just by the mention of your name, you are more powerful than anything. Donnie wants that power.

After that, Donnie starts doing little jobs for the wise guys. Gopher-type stuff that the rookie's rookie does. Smash a window, burn a car, slash a tire, deface a store front—shit like that. Not long after Donnie almost got arrested for driving Vinny Ruge's Lincoln is his first real arrest.

One night, Donnie gets told by Sally Two to go jump a few cars. Their cars have been sitting on the street for two days and no one has touched them, and they were taking up valuable parking spots for customers of Mikey's bar. Sally Two even gives Donnie a matchbook and some old whiskey bottles full of gasoline and tells him, "Do what you want with them. Just don't get caught."

That night, around two in the morning, Donnie smashes in the windows, hops in, jumps the cars, and drives them away from Mikey's. There is a big, long stretch of highway that the city has been building practically right next to Delaware Avenue called Interstate 95, and it is being worked on about two blocks east of Mikey's. So Donnie drives under I-95 and parks the three or four cars there.

On the fourth car, Donnie carries his gasoline bottles in the backseat. Donnie places all four bottles into the car, making sure that the bottles don't break. After parking under the interstate, he lights the cars up, like an assembly line of arson. Down the line. One by one. Rip the match, strike it, toss it in the car. Rip the match, strike it, toss it. Rip, strike, toss. Rip, strike, toss.

By the time the fourth one lights up, the first looks ready to pop, so Donnie gets out of there as fast as he can. By the time he gets about a block away, he knows the cars blow soon; but Donnie isn't paying attention and runs right into a beat cop, walking around the neighborhood, billy club in hand and ready to beat the living shit out of Donnie for knocking him over. The beat cop starts screaming at Donnie hard, his voice echoing his head, a voice that reminded him of his father. Donnie watches the cop's veins bulge more and more out of his neck and forehead with every word he takes.

"What the fuck are you doing out, boy? Do you realize how late it is? Are you starting troub—"

Just then, the first one explodes, and the cop looks right at Donnie and knows it was him. Donnie is sweating so hard, it looks like he's pissing himself. The cop stands up over Donnie and takes a quick whiff of him.

"Gasoline? What the fuck are you doing with gasoline at two in the morning?"

Donnie doesn't say anything. He can't, but even if he could, he wouldn't have. Donnie remembers Sals, one of the capos, telling him that if he ever wants to be a wise guy, the one thing that he must absolutely do is that he must never rat on his friends. For anything and about anything. Whether they did it or not is irrelevant. You never rat on your friends. Donnie gets pinched running back from a job he knows he did by a beat cop that knows he did it. But Donnie keeps his mouth shut. Donnie waits for his lawyer and the court case and gets to work. He still remembers that court case.

November 3, 1965. Donnie is sixteen years old, and the guys are able to get the best lawyer to help Donnie out. The jury is made up of ten white guys and two black guys, which some people didn't like, but Donnie didn't think that much about it. He was never a racist, so he didn't care. Donnie pleads the fifth for everything. They find no evidence of Donnie in the act of burning those cars.

According to the lawyer, Donnie just so happened to smell of gasoline on an early Saturday morning when Donnie decided it was a good time to go for a run and happened to stumble upon a suspicious police officer. The jury votes Donnie not guilty, and Donnie leaves the courtroom with a sense of victory. His first court case is beat, and it will not be his last.

As Donnie leaves the courtroom and walks into the hallway, he gets congratulated by all of the wise guys. Everyone is there: Books, Sals, Vinny Ruge, Tino, Mick, Sally Two, Badger, and Nicky Sweeps. It is like a fuckin' birthday party in the hall of the courthouse. Donnie is getting pats on the back, kisses on the cheeks, handshakes, fist bumps, the whole nine yards. After working through a sea of congratulatory wise guys, his adoptive father, Enzo, is right there to give Donnie a hug and congratulate him on his case. Donnie, spotting his dad, steamrolls toward him into his arms in a large hug.

"Pops! What are you doing here?"

"Whatta mean what am I doing here? You're my son, I always support my son."

Then, to Donnie's surprise, the wise guys all start moving single file in Enzo's direction, giving him a firm handshake or hugging him, which Enzo accepts generously.

"You know these guys?"

Enzo's face lights up with slight surprise. He assumed Donnie knew, but Enzo assumed wrong.

"Of course I know these guys, Donnie. They all work for me."

Donnie double takes between his adoptive father and the crowd of wise guys in the courthouse.

"I thought you just sold newspapers?"

Enzo couldn't help but let out a loud roar of laughter, the wise guys eventually joining in the laughter.

"I do much more than sell newspapers."

In that moment, Donnie's head implodes with thoughts. He couldn't believe it. Every time one of the guys mentioned "the Don," "the Man," "the Boss," or "the Big Guy," they were talking about Enzo, his adoptive father. Donnie had spent months and months dreaming about what the head of the family looked like, and he was living with him the whole time. After taking a few minutes to think,

Donnie's face erupts into a large smile, full of newfound appreciation for his adoptive father.

They all leave the courthouse, and Enzo puts a hand over Donnie's shoulder and starts talking to him, this time in a much more serious tone.

"You did good today, Donnie. You took it like a man. You've made me and all the guys proud."

"Thanks, Pops."

"I want you to start working with these guys a little more. Still do as they say, but you'll be into some more serious activities. If you're ready for it. I don't want to pressure you or nothing, Donnie."

His face lights up. He looks like a kid on Christmas. He couldn't stop smiling. "Absolutely. Anything for you, Pop."

Enzo smiles back at Donnie and gives him a quick hug before pulling away and patting his shoulder once.

"That's my boy."

From that point forward, Donnie starts working more and more with the wise guys, but with that, Donnie starts going to school less and less, his grades getting worse and worse. Donnie never finishes his junior year of high school. He gets expelled, and all Donnie is doing is protecting Ronan.

V

That Godforsaken Jungle

It is after school on his junior year of high school, and Ronan is a freshman. Donnie knows Ronan didn't get along well with the other kids, but he didn't know how severe it was. Normally, Once school is let out, Jamey and Ronan would wait outside for Donnie, and they'd all walk to Bruno's together. But instead of walking directly to Mikey's, Donnie and Jamey would walk Ronan home first and then head to Mikey's and work with the wise guys. One day, Donnie walks outside, and all Donnie sees is Jamey. Confused, Donnie walks up to Jamey and questions him about Ronan.

"Jamey, where's Ro?"

Jamey just shrugs and gives him a look.

"No clue, Donnie. I didn't even see him come out front."

When Jamey says that, Donnie knows exactly where Ronan is. There are only two ways to exit school, the school front and a back-door that leads to a small concrete lot that houses a maintenance shed and a garbage container. Nobody goes out the back unless they are headed for the maintenance shed. It had been used during Donnie's first year of high school, but since then, they moved the maintenance guys indoors and the shed sat empty in the lot for the last two years.

But ever since it closed, kids started having after-school fights in the shed. It is a pretty sizable shed. It can hold about fifteen to twenty kids in it but only about two to three are fighting at a time, so many

25

are just bystanders. Donnie has had his share of fights in that shed, and he's won all of them.

Donnie is a big kid. By the time he enters high school, he is about five foot five, 130 pounds of muscle because of his consistent athleticism, as well as still holding a large amount of pent-up aggression about his father who, by the time he started high school, is five years deep in his thirty-to-life prison sentence. Donnie is pissed at Ronan. He always watches over him. He is his baby brother. In an instant, Donnie drops his schoolbag and looks at Jamey with stone-cold eyes.

"Wait here. I'll be back in a few."

Donnie storms into the building, walks through the halls, and in a flash, is out the back door. The second he reaches the concrete lot, Donnie can hear a fight going on. He walks up to the shed and busts the doors open. It is all freshmen or sophomores, cheering on and chanting names. There are about twenty boys in the shed, with five boys in the inner circle fighting.

When Donnie opens the door, they all scatter like roaches, leaving the five boys in the shed all by their lonesome. One of the boys Donnie immediately recognizes is his baby brother Ronan. He is lying on the ground, his face swollen from punches, with blood running down his lips, nose, and cheeks, with a small gash above his left eye.

Donnie didn't hesitate a second. He rushes those four boys faster than they can react. He beats those kids. Donnie breaks a few noses and cracks one of the kids' femurs. Apparently, Donnie had broken one kid's nose so badly, he had to have numerous surgeries to replace the bones in his nose, as well as to fix his eye sockets and jaw, which had to be wired shut for two months. The kid who ratted him to the principal only got away with a busted jaw from one of Donnie's hooks to his face.

He dashes out of there, and Donnie feels like chasing him but has three other kids to take care of. He knocks all three of them out. It was pretty easy work, and he could've done it with one shot each. But Donnie wants to hurt them for hurting Ronan. After that, Donnie walks over to Ronan, who is sitting in the corner of the shed, curled up in a ball, crying into his knees. Donnie hasn't seen this kind of look since the day his old man got arrested. Donnie walks over to Ronan, and he looks up at Donnie, wiping his face of tears. Ronan is a mess.

"Why didn't you tell me, Ro? I could've taken care of these guys without you getting hurt."

Ronan starts tearing up again, speaking through a cracked voice.

"I don't know, Donnie. I thought I could take care of them myself. But it kept getting worse and worse, and then he told me to fight him and I didn't back down and..."

Donnie couldn't listen to him. Everything he is saying is getting jumbled together into one big mush of tears and incoherent words. Donnie leans down and gives him a big bear hug, which quickly suppresses his tears.

"I got you, Ro. From now on, I'll always have your back and I'll always protect you."

It is mid hug that the principal barges into the shed and spots all three boys with bloody faces knocked out cold on the shed floor. He rips into Donnie in an instant.

"What the hell is going on here, Mr. McCullough?"

Donnie is fuming. He stands up and rips into the principal himself.

"What's going on is my brother was getting beat up by these four boys, and I came in and defended him. That's what's going on."

Then, the principal starts saying something about not beating up the kids, that there's different ways to protect your brother. But then Donnie calls him a "fuckin' idiot," and the principal didn't like that. He gets sent home, being told his punishment will be dished out accordingly the next day. Donnie comes to school the next day to grab his things and is told not to come back. Donnie doesn't care. He shrugs at the principal and walks to Mikey's. Maybe he should've cared but he didn't. Regardless, even though he never went to school again after that, Donnie still watches over Ronan.

All the way to Vietnam.

In the fall of 1969, Donnie is twenty and Ronan is nineteen. They didn't want to wait and see if the draft would pick them. They always wanted to help their country in some way, and this seemed like the best option. Of course, Donnie doesn't want to leave behind the wise guys, but Donnie talks to Enzo about it and he says if he wants to, he'd be okay with that.

He is less worried about himself because of his dealings with the guys at Mikey's and more worried about Ronan and Jamey, who had spent some time around there but not nearly as much as Donnie and never did anything dangerous. All three of them enlist in early October 1969 and get shipped to boot camp on the fifteenth of the same month. They complete their training by January of 1970 and get shipped to Vietnam by February.

They didn't last long.

Jamey is in a different platoon than Donnie and Ronan. Jamey is shipped to Saigon to help control the attacks on the city. Donnie and Ronan, by some miracle of God, are placed in the same platoon, getting shipped to Cambodia. Donnie and Ronan barely last more than three months.

Donnie, Ronan, and two other guys are leading the platoon while trekking through the vast jungle environment of Cambodia when they get ambushed. Shots are cracking left and right over their heads and past the trees. Donnie drops to his stomach and starts firing his rifle as fast as he can. His men get hit and start dropping like flies. They get massacred.

Donnie crawls back to the platoon's heavy gunner's body, grabs his M-60, and lays down suppressing fire while yelling at what's left of the platoon to fall back into retreat. While running back, Donnie looks over at Ronan as he gets hit in the back, dropping down flat. In that instant, Donnie assumes the worst but hears him scream in agony, so he runs right back to him and gets him in a carry over his shoulders.

Donnie carries him for half a mile in retreat before they get air support from a Huey that sends the NVA running. They carry him back to the platoon base and lay him down in one of the trenches they've dug out. Donnie places him down on his back, but Ronan screams at him in pain. "Turn me on my fuckin' side, Donnie!"

Donnie turns Ronan on his side and takes a quick peer at his back, which is leaking blood slowly from bullet holes in his lower back and shoulder blades.

"Oh shit. You got hit, Ro."

"How bad, Donnie?"

"Bad, Ro. Looks like your back and shoulders. Can you wiggle your toes?"

Donnie watches Ronan look at him with fear as he looks down at his boots and tries to wiggle them. Once, twice, three times. Ronan is practically trying to will them to move with his mind but to no avail.

"I can't fuckin' move 'em, Donnie."

"Try your legs now."

Again, Donnie watches fear flood into his face like a bucket of cold water as Ronan tries to wiggle his legs. He can't. Donnie starts to panic.

"Okay, Ro. Can you move your arms?"

At this point, Ronan is on the verge of tears, but Donnie knows he trusts him. So Ronan does what Donnie says. Ronan looks at his hands and wiggles his fingers, then he flexes his wrists and rolls them around slowly. He moves his elbows seamlessly at the joints. The only problem Ronan has is moving his arms at the shoulder where he is shot at.

Donnie looks at Ronan's front side and sees two bullet holes, with blood flowing effortlessly from them. Donnie sheds a few fleeting tears of happiness before he sees no bullet holes on his stomach. The bullets are through and through on Ronan's shoulders but are lodged in his back. Donnie just looks at his baby brother, who is now crying tears of joy for being able to move his arms, and Donnie pats Ronan on his face.

"You're gonna be okay, Ro."

They have a medic on site, but Ronan needs professional medical help. He has bullets lodged in his backside and needs surgery to remove them, and from a field assessment done by Donnie and the doc, it looks like he is going to be paralyzed from the waist down if he even makes it out of there.

They spend fourteen days in that hellhole of a trench. All Ronan can do is lie on his side in writhing, agonizing pain. Ronan would cry himself to sleep silently every night for two weeks. Donnie stays by his side every single night and vows to stay until Ronan gets medevaced out of that godforsaken jungle.

After a week of waiting for help, the platoon discovers the base isn't safe enough to have a chopper land there, so they have to clear the forest before the medevac can arrive. It would take them months to clear the jungle. Ronan can't last months. Ronan doesn't last more than two weeks. With no foreseeable future of help or proper medical attention, Ronan's body caves.

While Donnie is asleep, Ronan, using solely his upper body, crawls about fifty yards and takes another Marine's service-issued M1911 pistol, crawls back over to Donnie, and taps him on the shoulder with the muzzle of the gun, whispering to wake Donnie up.

"Psst… Donnie. Donnie, wake up!"

After a few moments, Donnie finally swings around and looks at Ronan through blurry eyes. Donnie doesn't even see Ronan's face, but he sees the gun. Donnie rubs his eyes to make sure he isn't dreaming. Donnie looks at his baby brother like an absolute basket case, but Ronan is looking at Donnie with a look of complete, desolate sadness.

"Ro…the fuck are you doing?"

Ronan grabs the barrel of the gun and flips the pistol around, the handle facing Donnie's chest.

"I want you to shoot me, Donnie."

Donnie begins to feel anger form in his body, his face quickly growing beet red with rage.

"I'm not gonna fuckin' shoot y—"

"PLEASE, DONNIE!"

Ronan's voice is screaming whispers at Donnie, cracking with every word as tears start to roll down his cheeks.

"I can't take it anymore, Donnie. The pain is too much. I can't feel my feet. I can't feel my toes. I can't feel my legs. I can't feel fuckin' anything, Donnie. My back is slowly bleeding more and more. Every time I try and fall asleep, I can feel the bullets shift. Please, Donnie. You gotta do it."

Ronan shoves the handle of the pistol into Donnie's chest, and to prevent it from hitting, Donnie puts his hand up, half-grabbing the pistol. As Donnie fully grabs it, he watches Ronan slowly let go of the barrel, his arm collapsing to the dirt, his face covered with mixed emotions of sadness, anger, and pain.

"Make it look like I did it myself. Just hold up my arm and pull the trigger because I can't do it myself."

Donnie is in disbelief. Donnie can't shoot him. He's his baby brother. He can't. Donnie tosses the pistol a few feet away from him and grabs Ronan by his uniform collar, looking him dead in the eye with a stone-cold look.

"Ronan, you're my baby brother. I'm not fuckin' shooting you."

Donnie lets go of Ronan's collar, and his body sinks back into the dirt as Donnie sits back and looks at Ronan, his shock of the situation growing rapidly.

"If you don't shoot me… I'll scream. I'll scream so loud, you'll have to shoot me. Or those NVA motherfuckers will come racing to this camp and wipe us all out. I'll fuckin' do it, Donnie. I don't give a fu—"

Right then, Donnie snaps. Donnie had never laid a hand on his brother; but he socks Ronan right across the jaw, his face meeting the punch with incredible force and flying backward, flopping slightly after the punch. Donnie looks at Ronan, now bleeding harshly from his nose and mouth. Immediately, Donnie starts crying, just low enough to prevent waking the other soldiers.

"I'm sorry, Ro."

Ronan just looks at Donnie and smiles, blood slowly forming on his lips.

"It's okay, Donnie. I know you don't want to…but I need you to do this."

Donnie's head sinks into his chest. He peers over at the pistol, lying about four feet away in the soft dirt of the trench, staring right back at him. Donnie looks away but looks back a few seconds later.

After a minute or two of back-and-forth contemplation, Donnie crawls over and grabs the pistol out of the dirt.

He walks over to Ronan, looking up at Donnie with his bloody face, writhing with pain. Donnie grabs Ronan's hand, wrapping it around the handle of the gun, placing Ronan's index finger and Donnie's thumb on the trigger. Donnie starts crying as he moves the muzzle of the pistol and places it on Ronan's left temple, digging it in a little bit so Ronan's dripping sweat won't move the gun.

"You won't feel a thing, Ro."

"I know, Donnie. I know."

Through his tears, Donnie leans forward and kisses Ronan on the forehead, tasting his blood, sweat, and dirt on his chapped lips as he pulls away.

"I love you, Ronan."

"I love you too, Donnie."

Ronan doesn't feel a thing. Ronan doesn't have to worry about agonizing surgery or not being able to not walk again or the hellscape of the Cambodian jungle. Ronan is okay now. Ronan is okay.

As Donnie pulls the trigger, he watches Ronan's body slouch over at the waist, blood pouring from the gunshot wound. Donnie jumps back from the sound, standing up in fear and looks down, Ronan's hand still lifelessly clutching the pistol. Donnie drops on all fours and cries. He cries until the platoon captain comes running over with two men to investigate the origin of the gunshot. Once he sees Donnie, he stops running, takes his helmet off, and drops to one knee, placing his helmet over his heart in silent prayer.

VI

Bullet Holes and Blood Splatters

After everything happened in Cambodia, Donnie is relieved of his duties the next day and is sent home two days later to attend his brother's funeral. Donnie remembers his feet touching down stateside for the first time since February 15, 1970. Donnie gets home May 28.

Three months, one week, and six days.

Donnie doesn't even cry at Ronan's funeral.

Even though the doctor informed his mother and father of Ronan's supposed suicide by a gunshot wound, his mother insists on an open-casket viewing. Donnie looks at Ronan once at the viewing. From what Donnie sees, the morticians did a nice job covering up the gunshot. After that, Donnie doesn't look at him. Not even at the casket at the funeral. Donnie can't look at him. Donnie can't touch him. Donnie can't even get on his knees and pray from him. Donnie is too ashamed of himself.

It's hard going to someone's funeral knowing you put them there. Especially when you loved them. It's hard killing someone you love.

After that dreaded day, on May 25, 1970, Donnie became a stone-cold, heartless human. After Donnie got on all fours and cried harder than he ever cried before, he never cried again. He didn't cry at his funeral. He didn't cry at his burial. He didn't cry when he got home from the funeral. But boy, Donnie is angry.

After getting home from the funeral, Donnie tells Stella, his adoptive mother, that he is going for a quick drive to Mikey's. Donnie drives right back to the recruiter's office where he signed the papers in October not even four months ago and reenlists. Donnie goes back with a rage and a vengeance unparalleled to anything he had ever felt.

This is for his brother.

This is for Ronan.

Donnie signs the papers and gets sent back to Cambodia a week later. This time, they are tasked with cutting enemy communication lines in the everlasting Cambodian jungle. While clearing out an area a few miles outside of Phnom Penh, Donnie's platoon gets into a heavy firefight. While clearing out the jungle, the platoon leaves fox-holes in their path in case they need to get to cover quickly.

Once the NVA pop out, they hit the holes and return fire. Since Donnie had experience in Cambodia before, he is made point man of his platoon. If shit hits the fan, he is the first to hit the dirt and the last to stand up and most likely the first to die. But Donnie is a crack shot with the rifle. He let out three short bursts of his rifle, and moments later, three NVA soldiers dropped dead in the dirt.

But after a few minutes, the platoon gets overwhelmed and has to retreat. They fall back from foxhole to foxhole. It is an exhausting method but an effective one. Shoot, move, drop into a hole. Shoot, move, drop. Shoot, move, drop. But while moving back, through the incessant noise of gunfire and explosions, Donnie races into the next foxhole to check for enemies. After he checks it, he drops in and calls back for the platoon to follow. Just as Donnie calls back, an explosion goes off behind him.

He fears the worst. He waits a minute, and no one comes. Donnie peeks out of the foxhole, and a group of four NVA soldiers start barreling toward him, bayonets out and ready. Luckily, Donnie is able to let off a few short bursts, and they all drop in the foxhole dead. As one of them falls, Donnie ends up with a bayonet through his shoulder, going right through him like butter. As he peeks out again to see if more are coming, Donnie hears the almighty sound of chopper rotors and plane engines.

Anyone that is headed his way isn't coming anymore. One of the NVA soldiers Donnie thought dropped dead in the foxhole is still breathing and looks at Donnie with eyes full of pain and anguish. He is just a kid. Can't have been more than sixteen years old. Donnie looks at where he shot him, and there are two in his chest. He isn't lasting more than ten minutes. Donnie puts one between his eyes to end his suffering.

His body flinches backward, and his head droops slowly as the blood flows slightly down the bridge of his nose. Donnie unclips the bayonet from the rifle, the long knife still embedded in his body. As he crawls out of the foxhole, Donnie can see Hueys above him and tanks rolling up to him.

"It's all good, soldier! Let's get you the fuck outta here!"

"Oorah, sir!"

Donnie walks back to the foxhole where his men were at, waiting for his call. Donnie doesn't even walk all the way up to the hole before he sees the blood. Donnie creeps a little closer and sees one of his men's heads. Donnie walks away after that. He can't stomach it. He still has the knife in him and is losing his wits due to blood loss.

Donnie gets placed on a medevac and gets the knife taken out of him. Donnie needs about twenty-five stitches on both sides of his shoulder. Once Donnie gets home, he is home for good. He isn't going back. Nixon pulls the US out of the war in '73. Fifty-eight thousand men lose their lives. In three short years, Donnie's baby brother went from a soldier to a statistic. That's never a good way to see a person.

After Donnie gets back, he is twenty-one and a few months old. Donnie celebrated his birthday in that godforsaken jungle with a pack of cigarettes. When he gets back to Mikey's, it is like the Eagles winning the Super Bowl. Everyone is there: Enzo, Stella, Sals, Tino, Sally Two, Vinny Ruge, Books, Badger, Mick, Nicky Sweeps, and all the wise guys around. Apparently, a couple of the other families wise guys who knew their wise guys came along too.

Donnie sees a lot of faces at Mikey's he doesn't know when he gets back. When Donnie is talking to Nicky about it, Nicky says that Donnie is the only wise guy of the families to make it back. Donnie asks what happened to Jamey. Nicky's face furrows with sadness. Donnie looks at him again and asks what happened. He said they never recovered his body. Donnie nods once and taps Nicky on the shoulder. That's all he needs to hear. And all his body can take.

Donnie slugs back more alcohol that night than he ever had before. Perhaps because he could legally drink it now, but it was mostly in sadness for his brothers, biological or other. Donnie gets so drunk, Mick has to drive him home. Even though Donnie can barely see and is mumbling so bad, he sounds like an animal, Mick has plans that night; and let's just say him driving Donnie home isn't a part of them.

It is about two in the morning, and it is pitch-black. Not even the moon is out. After getting out of Mikey's, Mick, Nicky, and Donnie drive to another bar down Broad Street in the direction of city hall. They park out front of the bar and wait. At least a half hour passes before a group of three guys walk out of the bar and start making their way down the street.

After getting about a hundred feet in front of them, they start following behind them slowly in the car. After getting about two blocks, the three men hop into an old Buick and drive down the street, the trio of wise guys in pursuit. They drive for about half a mile before catching up to them at a red light. That's when the shots ring out.

Mick and Nicky both pull out pieces and shoot the car up. Donnie sobers up almost immediately. Gunshots are very sobering. Donnie looks up at the car, and all Donnie sees are bullet holes and blood splatters. Both Mick and Nicky empty their magazines and bolt down the street, turning after a few blocks to avoid any potential of police following them. Mick and Nicky dump their pieces in the Schuylkill and drive Donnie back to Enzo's house. Donnie crashes there and sleeps like a baby. Mick and Nicky's triple hit is about to tick off a family that shouldn't be ticked with, and Donnie is caught in the middle of it.

VII

Funny Guy

Ever since Donnie gets back from Vietnam, he is a horrific drunk. That's all he does. Donnie had hit a spur of depression. Because of Ronan, because of Jamey, because of life. Donnie had hit rock bottom. Donnie is coming home at two, three in the morning after doing jobs with the guys at Mikey's. Stella is getting more and more worried about Donnie. Enzo is getting worried too. Donnie had never Enzo as worried as what happened one night.

It is a long August night in 1972, a couple of years after Donnie got back and a few months after Mick and Nicky iced the three guys in the car. He is playing card games with Mick, Sals, and Nicky Sweeps in the basement gambling ring of the bar. Donnie is a master when it comes to rigging games. Donnie was never the smartest kid on the block, probably since he never graduated high school, but boy was he good at playing the games to his favor.

The basement had four card games: Mick would sit at the poker tables with Sals, Nicky would sit at the Texas Hold'em table, and Donnie would sit at the Blackjack table. The wise guys have young kids, most of them not even eighteen yet, run the tables like card dealers. Books is in charge of all four of them, watching over them like a hawk, making sure that the games, in one way or another, always lean in their favor. It was like their own little casino.

37

Most Vegas card dealers make less than thirty grand a year working five nights a week. Donnie is there two nights a week playing the card games at Mikey's, sometimes pulling two, three grand a night. After the night is over, they always put a hundred-dollar bill or two into the pockets of the dealers. Even when Donnie is drunk, he always remembers their smiles. They light up when that green hits their pockets.

After they wrap up the games, Donnie, Mick, Nicky, and Books stay after the bar closes down and play card games between themselves. Some of the kids stay after and serve the guys drinks, and if they are feeling ballsy enough, they'd hop in on a game or two.

One of the kids goes by the name of Joey Slur because of his racist tendencies toward Asian people due to him losing his brother in Saigon during the war. Ever since Donnie met him, they clicked. They always talk. About twenty, born in Philly, and raised by his Irish parents, Joey Slur is en route to be a good associate under Books and a fantastic wise guy.

Of course, since he isn't Sicilian, he couldn't be made, just like Donnie and Mick. Donnie and Mick loved Joey. They treat him like a little brother. Donnie loves Joey. He is good for business. He is humorous and isn't afraid to crack a joke or two, especially about the Asians. He doesn't care if you were born over there or born down the street from him. If you are of Asian descent, Joey hates your guts with a hatred so powerful, it drives him insane sometimes. They always end up laughing whenever he gets mad about them, and after the first few times, Joey realizes they are just joking with him and he'd laugh with them. Joey was the best.

It is a long night of gambling. Donnie is up about five or six grand, having the time of his life in Mikey's basement. After the bar is closed down, Donnie, Mick, Nicky, Books, and Joey Slur are staying after hours playing games. Donnie has a little bit of whiskey in his system but not enough to forget everything. Donnie only wishes he can forget that night now.

They are all playing poker. Just a few easy games. Of course, they are betting on it and trying to gain more money for themselves, but they wouldn't take these games as seriously as the bar games.

They played four games for about an hour, and the entire time, the table is sobering up with water and club sodas. Donnie is just getting started. He had slugged down half a bottle in half an hour, with more to come. Every hand Donnie had, every card that is dealt his way is losing him green. Donnie thinks he's going crazy. Every game he loses is just more whiskey in the system. Then, Joey starts making cracks at Donnie.

"Aye, Donnie. Maybe this just isn't your night."

"Ah bullshit. It wasn't my night when I got stabbed in the shoulder by the NVA. This is fuckin' nothing."

Joey starts laughing heartily.

"Yeah. Fuck those yellow-bellied gooks. Never had the balls to do anything. Tortuous motherfuckers. That's how they got Bobby. Captured him and they didn't give him any respect at all. Cut his head off and tossed it into the Mekong. Fuckin' bastards. Ma couldn't even have an open-casket funeral or look at her son one last time. She couldn't hide the embarrassment or the pain of looking at the top of a casket with a framed picture of Bobby in his Army uniform."

Joey sighs heavily. Like Donnie, he never cries anymore. Not after he lost his brother. He just hits the bottle. Same as Donnie, but Donnie is worse.

"Yeah. I remember when Ronan did it. Those bastards shot at our backs during retreat. No morality at all. Murderous motherfuckers. Ronan got hit three times in the back, and after two weeks of nonstop pain, he put a bullet through his head."

Mick is the only one who knows the true story. Donnie looks at Mick, and he nods somberly. Donnie looks at Joey, and he gives Donnie a smirk. Donnie didn't like that.

"What?"

"Nothing."

"No, what? You gave me a look. I'm just curious what you're thinking about."

Joey nods slowly and tries to brush the subject away, but Donnie persists.

"No, it's just a thought, Donnie. Don't take nothing of it."

Now, Donnie is really confused but more importantly, Donnie's getting mad. "Don't take nothing of what, Joey? I don't even know what you're fuckin' talking about."

Joey just sighs and wishes he stopped at the sigh. He doesn't. "Maybe your brother was a pussy."

Mick's jaw drops slightly in shock. He couldn't believe Joey just said that. Donnie places his cards face down on the table and leans back in his chair.

"How so, Joey?"

"Well… Bobby got his head cut off, but he died fighting for his country. Your brother succumbed to his pain. Didn't want to be there anymore. Couldn't handle it. Couldn't take it. Put one through himself. Like a pussy."

Donnie is livid. "No, maybe it was the fact that he was shot in the back three times and couldn't get medevaced outta there for another few months. Maybe it was the fact that he should've gone home that day, but he couldn't. Maybe it was the fact that after two weeks of agonizing pain, he realized that his life after this would be going nowhere. Maybe it was the fact that he saw himself as a burden to his fellow soldiers, especially me, who fuckin' cared for him day and night till he was gone. Maybe, maybe not. You weren't there but I was, so why don't you shut the fuck up and play the fuckin' game?"

The whole table is silent now. After Donnie finishes, they play cards for a few minutes before Joey gets up to get a drink. He turns around to look at the table, ready to make a snide remark geared at Donnie and Donnie alone.

"Anything for you, Mr. Donald McPussy?"

Immediately, Donnie begins laughing out loud. His guising laughter makes the whole table break out in thunderous roars of laughter as Donnie slowly reaches behind his jacket to the small of his back, pulling out his signature piece.

"You know, you're a funny guy, Joey."

After grabbing his club soda off the counter, Joey turns around while laughing hysterically, and Donnie never forgets the look on his face as he pulls the trigger.

The first three bullets hit Joey square in his chest, twice in his left breast and once in his sternum. The last three hit him twice in the neck and once in his nose. He drops like a sack of potatoes. Blood starts pooling up on the basement floor. His eyes are glued open, his face permanently covered with a look of shock and fear, with blood running out of his mouth and nose, and down his cheeks, lips, and jaw. The whole table jumps up at the sound of the shots and back away from the table. Nobody says a word to him, but everyone gives Donnie looks that say, What the fuck did you just do?

Donnie doesn't care.

In hindsight, he feels like an asshole, but he doesn't regret doing it. Ronan is no pussy. If anything, Donnie is the pussy. Donnie did it to him. Ronan wanted to die, but he couldn't have killed himself without Donnie. When Joey called Ronan a pussy, Donnie took it more as a personal insult. Regardless, after Donnie shoots Joey, Mick and Nicky stay at the bar to clean up the basement, with Books and Donnie getting rid of the body.

They wrap him in plastic and pour lye over his body to make sure it starts dissolving as they get to the river. Since Joey isn't a known associate, they didn't have to worry about taking him to the Dump and cutting him up. They drive out to the northeast and bury him along the Pennypack River.

They park off Frankford Avenue and walk down to the edge of the river. Donnie has dug a hole or two before, but Books is tired from the long night. It takes them about an hour or two to finish the hole; and they carry his plastic-wrapped, lye-covered body into the hole, burying him far from his Fishtown home.

After walking back to the car, Donnie tosses the shovels in the back and gets in the passenger seat. As Books is walking around to get in the driver seat, a car flies down the road and machine gun fire echoes through the night, spraying the upper half of the car. Donnie ducks down as soon as he hears the first shot. After two to three seconds of rapid-fire gunshots, Donnie hears the screech of car tires pull away from the car. Donnie slowly sits upright and follows the trails of bullet holes, leading from the back of the trunk through the backseat windows and through the top of the front seats.

If the bullets were a blade, it would've cut the top of the car clean off. While following the bullet holes, blood stains erupt into Donnie's sight as he sees Books slowly fall over, his chest, neck, and hands covered in blood. The driver-side window is open, so his lifeless hands grab onto the opening and look at Donnie with his dying eyes.

"Fuckin'…drive!"

After that, Books collapses on the road. Immediately, Donnie hops into the driver's seat and steams out of the northeast, looking at Books's dead body pooling with blood in the rearview mirror.

As Donnie makes his way back to Fishtown, the only thing going through his head is Who the fuck am I killing next?

VIII

I Disappeared or Disappeared

When Donnie gets back to Fishtown, he is dripping with sweat. It looks like Donnie had walked through a rainstorm. Mick and Nicky are waiting back at Mikey's for Donnie and Books to get back before they go home. They are sitting outside on the front steps, smoking cigarettes as Donnie pulls up to the bar front. Donnie pulls up so fast, he jumps the curb and almost runs into them.

They jump back and start cursing at Donnie as he jumps out of the car. "Yo, what the fuck, Donnie? You trying to fuckin' kill us here?"

"Shane's dead!"

Both of them stop immediately. "What?"

"Shane's fuckin' dead, Mickey! They shot the car up on Frankford. I was in the car when someone drove by and shot the car and Books up. He's dead!"

Mick and Nicky look at each other and look back at Donnie in fear. "Did you get a look at the guys?"

Donnie shakes his head. "No. Too dark, and I ducked once I heard the shots. I don't know how many were there, but it sounded like more than one gun."

Mick and Nicky look at each other again, this time with more fear. "Did you get a look at the car?"

Donnie snaps and punches the brick wall outside of Mikey's in anger, breaking his wrist. "I don't fuckin' know anything, Mick. Okay? Jesus Christ, Books is dead. It was dark, it was late, I was drunk. Stop talking to me like a fuckin' cop, all right?"

Mick waves his hand dismissively at Donnie and starts pacing in front of Mikey's. Nicky walks over to a payphone about ten feet outside of Mikey's and puts in a phone number. After a few seconds, Nicky grunts loudly and hangs up, the plastic receiver bashing down on the metallic hook switch. He walks back and peers at Mick, and almost instantly upon looking at him, a lightbulb goes off in his head.

"Mick, we gotta get the fuck outta here."

"Why?"

"If anything, I don't think it was a hit on Books. I think it was supposed to be a hit on you or me, but Books got hit 'cause he was with Donnie."

"What the fuck are you talking about?"

"What do you mean, what am I talking about? I'm talking about Mazzante, you dim-witted fuck. The three guys Enzo told us to hit. From Mazzante's crew. Donnie was the only other person who was in the fuckin' car that night."

Donnie is floored by what Nicky is talking about. "Wait a fuckin' second. The hit from months ago?"

Nicky nods once, looking around frantically for cars or people, afraid to be crept up on after Donnie's sudden appearance.

"That was the Mazzante crew? Are you fuckin' kidding me, Mickey? The fuckin' Mazzante family? Why did you do that?"

"We were told to by Enz…by your pops. Said three of Carlo's associates were creeping into our territory, trying to steal our moneymakers."

"Were any of them made, Mick?"

Mick sighs and nods, putting two fingers in the air.

"Jesus, Mick. You know the rules about made men. You don't touch them unless specified!"

"I know, Donnie. I'm sorry for getting you involved. But right now, me and Nicky are getting the fuck outta here."

Mick and Nicky hop into Mick's car and drive away from Mikey's. That is the last Donnie ever hears from those two. Donnie thinks maybe they are out on the lam to stay safe. Donnie never saw them again.

Donnie always wonders if they disappeared or disappeared.

Guess he'll never know for sure.

IX

Heaven on Earth

Callen Mahony walks down the alleyway, hands shaking and ears ringing slightly. He doesn't even look back at him. He knows he's dead. After exiting the alleyway, he gets into a car, which drives away speedily down the street, as Callen wipes the droplets of blood off his face.

A few minutes' drive, and he's back at the headquarters. He walks in around midnight on a Tuesday night when the place isn't exceptionally busy. After entering, he veers left and walks four booths down, met with the sight of a portly man with thinning hair, smoking a cigar with a bottle of bourbon next to his glass, which is full of ice and alcohol.

"Billy's gone for good."

The man grunts once, sticks the cigar in his mouth, takes a few quick puffs, and smiles at his son.

"That's my boy."

"Anything for my father. And my Don as well."

Don Mahony smiles and taps his son on his shoulder. After a few taps, he stands up and embraces his son with a hearty hug. Callen almost shit himself shooting Billy. He was his best friend. But the Don needed him gone. He did what he had to do.

Micheal Cian Mahony was born on January 24, 1910, in the slums of Dublin, Ireland. He is born into an impoverished family, the youngest of five children and two struggling parents. Even in poverty, Micheal is considered very lucky. Despite his family's poor financial situation, his parents love each other and their children very much, providing everything they have for them, whereas most families Micheal knows only has one parent or lived with their grandparents.

From a very young age, Micheal recognizes the daily struggles of his family, seeing their lack of money or food on the table. Regardless of how his parents work, they would make sure their children always eat, even if that means they don't. Micheal's parents would sometimes go two, three days without a meal. By eight years old, Micheal's father is laid off his job at the metal plant.

That is the first time Micheal saw his father cry. He cries not because of his job or because of the money; he cries at the thought of his children going hungry or getting sick due to lack of nutrition needed. From this point on, Micheal makes a promise to himself that he will do whatever is necessary to provide for his siblings but, more importantly, his parents.

Micheal hates his name, so when the neighborhood boys begin to call him "Mickey," he is very pleased. Mickey meets up with three to four other children of his age and, using long coats that run down to their ankles, walks into stores and steals food off the shelves. They cleverly called themselves the Long Coat Gang; and very soon, more and more children join his gang, with more and more families suddenly getting food on their tables, not only for their siblings but their parents as well. The longer the gang stands, the more experienced they become.

After doing this for five years, at the age of thirteen, Mickey and the Long Coats move on from stealing food to stealing goods. Anything from socks to radios to jackets—whatever Mickey and his gang can get their hands on—they steal. Mickey and a few members would go into the more affluent areas of Dublin and rob trucks.

Since they don't have guns, they would cover their hands in hand towels, giving the drivers the illusion of a gun. They stick the towel in the driver's face, who would subsequently get out of the truck, and then they would steal the truck, leaving the driver on some pitch-black road with no means of getting home or back to work. They would continue to do this until Mickey's eventual first arrest.

He is on a job with three other boys, and he is holding up a truck that is supposed to be filled with a hundred designer jackets and dresses. Mickey stops the driver, tells him to roll down his window, and then sticks the paper bag in his face. The driver gets out of the truck, and in a scared voice that catches Mickey off guard, he screams at the top of his lungs, "Everything's in the back! Just please don't shoot me!"

Now Mickey has heard this line a million times before, from newbie drivers to drivers that have been trucking for thirty years.

This time, something is different in his tone.

Nevertheless, Mickey, with his towel-covered hand placed a few inches away from the man's back, tells him to open the back. Just as the man breaks the door seal, the truck shifts and Mickey's heart drops. Twenty policemen armed to the teeth with shotguns and revolvers jump out of the truck.

By the time they jump out, all three boys with Mickey are racing out of the alleyway and away from the cops. The majority of the cops ran after the boys, eventually losing them as they reached the seemingly everlasting slums. Mickey is tried as an adult and gets beat by the judge, charged, and convicted to jail for three years for armed robbery. He didn't even have a gun.

Mickey is sent to Dublin Penitentiary which, for the average prisoner, is the epitome of hell. But for those who have the dough or the influence, it is heaven on earth. Jail changes Mickey, but in his first three days, it changes from a hellhole to a slice of heaven in Ireland. All because he meets the son of Irish boss, Joey "Murph" Murphy, son of Don Thomas "Bullet" Murphy.

Murph, six years Mickey's elder at nineteen years old, has heard of the Long Coat Gang and is very impressed at how much Mickey has grown a following and how much power he's held in the five years he ran the gang. Mickey curiously asks Murph how he ended up in the slammer. Murph said he was caught robbing a clothing store in Limerick.

At least he had a gun when he did it.

Murph borrows his father's car for "an errand," he drives to Limerick, sticks the store up, and dashes out with the cash. He gets caught because on his way out the store, he runs right into a beat cop. He got sent back to Dublin Penitentiary and is currently serving six years.

Almost instantly, Murph and Mickey click. Murph, with the influence of his father, is able to cut his sentence in half with bribes; but even more importantly, Murph introduces Mickey to the real lifestyle of a gangster. He gets him inside what most prisoners call the House. It is basically this dormitory-esque building where all the mob guys stay for their sentences. All they have to do is pay the dough, and they are in. In his first week in jail, Mickey goes from your everyday Joe Schmoe to the newest member of the Murphy crime family.

In three years, he talks to every mobster in the family, from soldiers to capos to even Don Murphy's own underboss, Seamus "Mac" MacDonlevy. Through his close friendship with Murph, he begins forging friendships with the soldiers, many who are there for petty crimes—burglarizing, racketeering, and the likes—but some men are there for much more severe crimes such as murder and arson, serving minimal sentences due to lack of evidence, bribery, or a little bit of both.

Mickey is scared of those men, but Murph would usually hang around the men who killed and he often explains to Mickey that it takes a certain man to kill. It takes loyalty, guts, and a whole lot of crazy to do something like that. Murph also characterizes the hit men that work for his father as artists. They could be as creative or as simple as they wanted to be as long as what they did sent the message.

By the time he is sixteen, Mickey is out of jail and hanging out regularly with the Murphy crime family. He begins seeing his parents less and less, and his parents want to see less and less of him, seeing how much jail has changed their sweet baby boy. His life of crime begins pushing him away more and more; and one day, when he is around eighteen years old, he comes home at three in the morning and his father is waiting there, belt in one hand and empty whiskey bottle in the other.

"I'm sick and tired of the lack of respect you have for your mother and me. You and me. We're gonna settle this. Right here. Right now."

Mickey, smoking a cigarette, flicks the butt on the floor and crushes it underneath his sole. His father drops the bottle and comes charging at his son like a raging bull. Mickey steps to the side and hits his father once on the face, square in the jaw, knocking him to the ground. His father, fuming, turns around on his knee to face Mickey, only to be met with the sight of his youngest son holding a gun at him, the barrel only a few inches from the bridge of his nose.

"Don't you fuckin' tell me what I can or can't do. I did everything for you, and this is the thanks I receive?"

A noise upstairs causes Mickey's face to run cold. His mother is standing at the top of the steps, wrapped in a bathrobe, crying. His father shouts up the steps. "Go to bed, Mary!"

"What's wrong, Thomas? I heard some noises and I decided to—"

"I said go the fuck to bed!"

His father's voice, filled with anger and pain, scares Mickey a little bit; but he shakes the thoughts away and stares his father down, who is now crying slightly, tears falling onto the aged wooden living room floor.

"I'm never coming back. This is the last you will see of me. I'm packing a bag, and then I'm gone for good."

Mickey slowly brings the pistol down and places it in his waistband, walking upstairs to pack a bag. After packing, he walks downstairs and out the door. He hasn't seen his parents since.

That was in 1928.

By 1930, the Murphy crime family decided to move to the States, landing in the port of Augustine in May of 1930, moving up the coast and eventually settling down in the City of Brotherly Love by Christmastime. They quickly make their mark in the city, jutting out petty street gangs and forming their larger and more sophisticated crime family. They no longer worry about stealing jackets and coats, as there was a much more lucrative business in trade—bootlegging.

Though they came much later after the passing of the Eighteenth Amendment, in those three short years between 1930 and 1933, they turned Philadelphia into the leading city of booze and liquor on the coast. Hundreds of thousands of containers and boxes would go in and out of the city in a week, with the Murphy crime family in the front. They would buy up acres and blocks of city property to build speakeasies and secret bars, all the while paying off the beat cops to look the other way. The Murphy crime family transforms from a bunch of Irish immigrants with a background of crime to a multi-million-dollar criminal organization, all in the matter of three short years.

During those years, Mickey moves very quickly up the ranks, going from a lowly twenty-year-old soldier to a captain before he was even twenty-four. Since Philadelphia is right on the river, they can easily ship liquor up and down the Delaware, to New York, Baltimore, and even going west to Pittsburgh and Cleveland. Mickey shows his unceasing loyalty to Don Murphy by pulling off extravagant murders, burning the competition to the ground with Molotov cocktails and becoming an expert at his niche in the mob, kidnapping.

Mickey would find out people from gangs and mobs who have strong ties to their rival dons and he kidnap them, but Mickey isn't your run-of-the-mill kidnapper. He doesn't, initially, hold a ransom for their men. On the first go-around, he kindly asks the rival bosses for a small section of turf in exchange for their men back. Unlike money, which can be remade in days or even hours depending on the amount, turf is different. Your turf is your turf. You will do anything to protect your turf against your impending rivals.

Most bosses, due to either arrogance or apathy, do not comply with Mickey's demands, which makes his job easier. He keeps them until their bosses grow anxious enough to either get a new person for the job or ask how much. Mickey wouldn't kidnap high-level employees until much later in his gangster career, but he would kidnap people important enough for their empire to grow anxious.

He'd kidnap people every day, sometimes in groups with the help of the other captains. Mickey is an artist at this. He whittles away at the turf or grows the money until their territory is small enough to take or they have enough to whack the gang as a whole. In two years, by the time he is thirty, after gaining control over all of the northern sections of Philadelphia, Don Murphy passes down his reign to his ever-loyal captain, Mickey Mahony.

About five years after becoming boss, on November 10, 1945, Don Mahony drunkenly makes a ludicrous sports bet, betting the deed to a small family bar in Fishtown right on the border between his territory and the ever-growing Sicilian crime organization. This bet is between Don Mahony and an up-and-coming Philly Boss, Enzo Giambruno.

Enzo Giambruno haphazardly meets Mickey Mahony at the bar, having a few drinks while they talk business. During that time, a college football game is going on between Army and Notre Dame. Army is ranked first in the nation, with Notre Dame at second. Just as the game starts, Mickey asks Enzo who is going to win the game. Enzo, without expression, says that Army will crush the Fighting Irish.

Mickey scoffs at Enzo blasphemously. In an incredibly drunk state, Mickey proposes a bet. If Notre Dame wins, Enzo will fall under Mickey's reign, acting as informants for the Sicilian crime organization. Enzo agrees but states if Notre Dame loses, Enzo wins the deed to the bar. Both parties do the gentleman's shake and watch the game with fervent joy.

Notre never even scores a point in that game, the Black Knights shutting out the Fighting Irish 48–0. Mickey has no choice but sign the deed of the Mikey's Bar over to Enzo Giambruno, who has since made it his headquarters and home gambling ring. After losing the bar, Mickey Mahony makes a silent treaty between himself and a Philly boss, Angelo Mazzante, this agreement known famously as the Mahony-Mazzante Treaty.

This treaty will last for decades until one of Mickey's captains whacks the boss himself and gives away all Mahony territory to the Mazzante organization in exchange for full protection to run his drug-smuggling operations. Eventually, his drug operations were taken over by the much more powerful and ruthless Mazzante family.

X

The Power of Four

Donnie never grew fond of Mickey Mahony. When he heard he got whacked, by his own captain nonetheless, Donnie shed no tears for the man. In his eyes, Mickey had his respect, but that treaty is probably the worst thing he could've done for the Philadelphia crime families, Irish, Sicilian, or otherwise. Teaming up with the Irish gangs under Mickey Mahony practically made Angelo Mazzante a monarch of the Philadelphia underworld. Of course, other than Mickey Mahony, there are other bosses outside of Philly that Angelo is partnered with.

There is Miami boss Sandro Tadolini. He runs the drugs. From cocaine to methamphetamines, Don Tadolini does it all. He used to be a local drug runner for a cartel in Guadalajara, but he fled for personal reasons unbeknownst to the other dons. He set up shop in Miami and began running drugs all over Southern Florida.

That's when he meets Angelo Mazzante.

They met at a dinner where the local drug businesses meet to discuss big packages. Don Mazzante conducts the meeting because of the size of the package. And this package is big. The package is estimated at eleven thousand kilos of pure H, supposedly hitting Naples Beach in two days, with another ten thousand kilos of cutting substances to be shipped to Miami the following day.

Don Tadolini is instructed to pick up the substances package, and Don Mazzante will pick up the H from Naples Beach. From there, they will meet in a secret warehouse that only Don Mazzante knows about. Rumor has it it's somewhere in the Everglades, but Don Tadolini never believes anything he isn't told about from the source. After the warehouse meeting, there will be cutters chosen by Mazzante himself. They did their job perfectly because of the cut they will receive.

They wouldn't receive cash. They would receive dope.

The cutters take the coke, dump it out, and mix it with the cutting agents. The agents range anywhere from baking soda to sugar to cyanide but mostly just the first two unless you want to wipe out a city of junkies. After cutting it, it is to be repackaged and set to look like new. With such an extensive package, the cutters have their work made out for them.

It takes a team of five cutters two weeks to work through everything. When they are done, there is over twenty-three tons of dope. After mixing and cutting and repackaging, the cutters are worn down to the core. This is when Don Tadolini meets the ruthless side of Angelo Mazzante. After loading the trucks with the H, the cutters are taken out behind the warehouse to the shipping container that supposedly held their dope.

Mazzante murders them on the spot. Two of his soldiers dig graves and bury them behind the warehouse. Don Tadolini is sitting inside the warehouse when the gunshots ring out. He stands up to leave, but Mazzante walks through the door, cutting Tadolini off. Mazzante, clutching a .45 in his right hand, saunters slowly over to Tadolini. Mazzante motions Tadolini to sit, and he does.

Mazzante is pacing back and forth in front of Tadolini, the smell of gunpowder eking off his blood-sprayed shirt and jacket. Mazzante stops to face Tadolini, his face emotionless. He stares intently at Tadolini, and after a minute or two, he opens his jacket and holstered the gun.

"You're a good don, Sandro. I would like to work with you. Help you build your empire. I understand that you control most of the drugs that are provided around Southern Florida. If you would like my help and the help of my teamsters, we could run Florida and the south in its entirety. Take this as my favor to you, as you've helped me generously with my movement of the package."

Don Mazzante walks over to Don Tadolini and sticks his hand out. Tadolini stands up, meeting eye to eye with Mazzante. After a few moments of silence, their handshake seals their partnership and the start of a friendship between Angelo Mazzante and Sandro Tadolini. After this handshake, Tadolini becomes as unstoppable and as ruthless as his fellow don and now best friend, Angelo Mazzante. Now, Don Tadolini runs drugs all over the country, all through the help of don.

Don Camillo Maggio is another of Angelo's Mazzante list of partners. He is the New Orleans mob boss. Don Maggio runs the casinos from Atlanta to El Paso. Every single one of them. Though not on paper, Don Maggio is a silent partner in one way or another in every casino in the south. He always gets his piece of the deal. Along with the casinos, he runs multiple prostitution rings in New Orleans and all of Louisiana, which was his start-up job as a young Sicilian adolescent in the south.

Around seventeen at the time, a young Camillo Maggio is struggling to help his single mother and his two brothers with money, as they are in the heart of the Great Depression. They live in a small slum apartment in downtown New Orleans. His father had left his mother when his youngest brother, Salvatore, was just a baby. Camillo was about seven years old.

Now at seventeen, he is an errand boy for the neighborhood grocer, and at nights, he is a bouncer at a nightclub. Even as a young boy, Camillo was big. He was tall and built, not fat but not lean either. Even without working out, he would always wake up and go for early morning runs, finishing them with numerous sets of push-ups and sit-ups.

Now at seventeen, he stands at five foot ten, 190 pounds of pure muscle. As a bouncer, he is always able to make a little side money here and there. If a man wants to go into the back room with one of the girls, Camillo gives the man his price, and nine times out of ten, he is able to front the cash. The men would slip the money in Camillo's shirt pocket, and he would open a door to a secluded room.

"You got thirty minutes."

And off they were to do their business.

The owner of the nightclub always had a liking for Camillo. One night, after the nightclub was dying down, the owner walks up to Camillo and asks him to join him in his office. Camillo never knew his boss' name. Nobody did but everyone who knows him always respectfully called him Mr. Saint, so that's what Camillo called him. Camillo walks into Mr. Saint's office and sits down in his chair, looking around the room, which is covered in newspapers clippings, articles, and front-page headlines of Mr. Saint's face, with headlines reading things like "MOB BOSS BEATS MURDER CASE" and "RAZOR CACCHIONE ACQUITTED OF RACKETEERING CHARGE."

This is the day future Don Camillo Maggio finds out who his boss truly is, New Orleans mob boss of the time, Salvatore "Razor" Cacchione.

Don Cacchione ran the casinos, gambling, prostitution, drugs, guns, and everything in between as mob boss of New Orleans. Beginning his era of reign after the end of World War II, Don Cacchione was a ruthless businessman. Instead of having his soldier or his caporegimes place hits on people he didn't need or didn't want in his territory, he would have his men kidnap them and bring them back to various locations unbeknownst to everyone except his caporegimes. There, he would then deal with his troubles himself.

How painful or painless the death of his enemies depended on how severe the damage was to Don Cacchione and his businesses. If it was a slap on the wrist but an inexcusable slap, Don Cacchione would make their death quick and painless. A simple bullet between the eyes, and off he was to his next business deal. But if it was serious damage against the don, especially his casino business, he would make them bleed.

Rumor has it that Don Cacchione once cut a man by the name of Mr. White. He was the owner of one of Don Cacchione's casinos in El Paso. Turns out, Mr. White was stealing money from the casino and rigging games to his favor. Even though he was the owner, it was Don Cacchione's money. He feels very strongly about his money.

He covered him with papercut-thin cuts, just enough to make him bleed ever so slightly. While that doesn't sound bad, he had him stripped naked and covered his body, head to toe, the small cuts slowly driving Mr. White insane.

After about forty-five minutes of torture, he snapped. Mr. White let out a scream so bloodcurdling, it awoke Cacchione's driver who was sitting outside the warehouse. Midscream, Don Cacchione slit his throat, blood spitting from the wound and covering the don's jacket. The don, after wiping his face and jacket of his blood, smiled and watched slowly as he bled to death in the chair. His caporegimes then wrapped his body up and disposed of him in the Mississippi.

That was one time.

Don Cacchione got indicted and convicted of seventeen murders, as well as a long rap sheet of theft, fraud, extortion, racketeering, and much more. According to his caporegimes, Mr. White's murder wasn't even the worst one.

Don Cacchione died in '72 in prison right before the US pulled out of Vietnam.

No one knows how he died in prison, but it was ruled a suicide. How you end up breaking your nose while hanging yourself is a question nobody dares to ask. What's done is done.

Having no children, Don Cacchione's underbosses serve in his place before leaving his entire empire to a man who had been learning the ropes since the young age of seventeen. That was the day Camillo Maggio became the new don of New Orleans.

There is New York boss Alfonso Gamberini. Don Alfonso Gamberini's partnership with Dom Mazzante seems like the perfect fit to the puzzle. Both of them function in the northern unions, and they figure out quickly that it is better if they worked together instead of against each other. They met one day in Las Vegas, and their friendship and partnership became sealed.

Together, these four gentlemen control everything from drugs to unions to gambling to prostitution and sex rings. Through these rackets, they become the most powerful figures in the States. More powerful than the president. More powerful than anyone.

XI

Up the Chain

After Mick and Nicky leave that night, Donnie goes home. It is late when Donnie walks in, about four thirty in the morning. Stella doesn't usually stay up, but this time, she does. She is worried. The second Donnie opens the door, she is right there waiting for him.

"Where were you, Donnie? I was worried sick about you."

"I was at Mikey's with Mick and Nicky." Donnie gets choked up for a second, but he hides his cracked voice well. "And Shane. We were having drinks and shooting the shit. Lost track of time. Sorry Momma. Won't happen again."

Donnie starts walking toward the stairwell when he stops himself. "Is Pops up by any chance? Did he talk to you about anything?"

"You know my Enzo. As far as business, he doesn't tell me anything. Anyways, he's upstairs on the phone. He told me to wait downstairs when I woke up."

Even though she doesn't like it, she deals with it. Donnie loves Stella. Donnie walks over to her, gives her a peck on the cheek, and heads upstairs to Enzo's room. Donnie knocks once on the large wooden door and hears a few quiet footsteps creep slowly toward the door. Quietly, the door opens to a crack, the few inches of space showing only a partial face. After a small moment of recognizing who it was, Enzo opens the door fully and gives Donnie a hug. They sit down at a small table ten feet away from the bed and begin talking.

"Did'ya hear?"

"Yeah. Nicky called me. Are he and Mick on the lam?"

"Yeah. I was right fuckin' there. My ears are still ringing. Can't believe it was Books, Pops. He didn't have a violent cell in his body. Fuck!"

Donnie slams his fist on the table in anger, further worsening the extent of the break.

"Jesus, I think it's broken."

Enzo stands up and looks at his son's wrist, now hanging limply at the joint. Enzo turns his wrist to look at his watch and sighs heavily.

"Ah shit. Put some ice on it and get some sleep. We'll go to the hospital tomorrow and then Mikey's right after. Our informants are coming around eleven. Apparently, they got someone already."

Enzo leans over and gives Donnie a kiss on each cheek. "I love you, Donnie."

"Love you too, Pops."

After that, Donnie leaves the room, heading down the hall to his bedroom and falling asleep in a minute.

After shutting the door, Enzo walks over to a small cupboard and opens it, grabbing a bottle of red wine out of it. He opens it and pours himself a glass. After returning the bottle to its original location, he raises the glass to his lips and downs it in one swig. After that, he hops into his bed and falls asleep quickly, only interrupted by the sound of his wife entering a few minutes later. Enzo slept well that night. He always sleeps well when there's business to take care of. Business he's dealt with since he was just a small boy in the slums of Sicily.

Enzo Stefano Giambruno grew up in the poverty-stricken slums of Palermo, Sicily, after being born on Christmas Day, 1905. The third child of eight children, Enzo is the oldest and only boy of the family, always watching out for his younger siblings.

Being the oldest, at a very young age, he is forced into being the man of the house, often cooking, cleaning, and working for his family. When his father abandons his family in 1914, Enzo is only nine years old. From that point forward, his mother relies on him to help provide for the family. His mother would work during the day as a nurse for the Italian Army as it entered the Great War, sometimes making no more than a few dollars for close to twelve hours of work. Enzo starts going into the city and doing a multitude of jobs, from shining shoes to delivering newspapers to bagging items at the local shops. Most importantly, Enzo starts to sell war bonds.

After growing up in the slums for ten years, Enzo runs into a boy that he eventually becomes good friends with. His name is Luca Ricci. Luca's father owns a printing press. His father takes sheets of paper and prints out the war bonds by the hundreds every single day. His son and Enzo would then go out and sell them for five to ten dollars each.

They would mature for ten years, and once those ten years came up, they would cash them in. Enzo and Luca would sell close to two hundred war bonds per day, totaling anywhere between one to two thousand dollars. Mr. Ricci isn't very generous with his money but had agreed with his son Luca that Enzo would receive one percent of the weekly profits of the war bonds.

Enzo would easily make a hundred dollars a week selling the bonds and every week. He would come home with enough food for the family to fill everyone's stomachs for that week. Enzo would then save whatever money is left over from food buying and put it in a small leather pouch that he has next to his bed. After working for around two months, Enzo walks into the shop one day and places the leather pouch on the table. Mr. Ricci looks slowly at Enzo, confused by what he wants to do.

"I want to buy some war bonds for my family."

Mr. Ricci's heart sinks in his chest.

"I'm sorry, Enzo, but you cannot buy the war bonds."

Enzo is confused and upset with Mr. Ricci. Enzo knows that Mr. Ricci is greedy, but Enzo truly didn't realize the extent of his job.

"Why can't I buy war bonds?"

Mr. Ricci starts to sweat. He doesn't want to tell him the truth. "Because you can't and that's that. Get out of my shop and do your job!"

Mr. Ricci snaps at Enzo who, even at ten years old, is shocked at how frightening his voice becomes. He runs out of the shop, crying slowly, and Mr. Ricci's heart sinks even more. He whispers quietly to himself as he walks back to the printing room. "I can't tell him the truth. I just can't."

After running out of the shop, Enzo quickly wipes his tears and meets up with Luca on one of the many busy streets that they frequented to sell their war bonds. Still upset but mostly furious, Enzo picks up a stack of bonds and starts selling them with Luca, who quickly picks up on his upset demeanor.

"The hell's wrong with you?"

"I tried to buy some bonds, but your dad won't let me. What reason does he have not to let me buy them? I've been busting my ass to provide for my family for the last year. I've sold tens of thousands of his bonds with you, and all he does is print them. He's not out here with me or you selling them. In the heat. In the rain. In the snow. We're out here busting our balls for fourteen hours every day, and he's inside his shop like a recluse, basically printing money for himself."

Luca nods his head, agreeing with Enzo but eventually shakes his head and gets back to work.

"I get where you're coming from, Enzo, but I can't. He's my father. I gotta help him."

Enzo is fuming now. He throws his stack of bonds and kicks over the remaining piles. "Fuck this and fuck you. I'm out of here."

Enzo turns away from Luca, who is now on all fours picking up the piles of bonds, looking up in tears to see his friend walking away. After walking a few blocks away, Enzo starts to cry and begins running home. While racing home in his tear-filled fit, he accidentally runs into a man, who is dressed so nicely it seems to repress his crying. The man doesn't budge, but Enzo falls over after hitting the man. Enzo, now on his knees, turns his face parallel to the ground to look at the man.

The man looks like Sicilian royalty. Average height but portly in figure, standing at five foot seven but two hundred pounds, dressing in an impressive three-piece suit, with designer shoes and a gold watch wrapped perfectly around his left wrist. He turns around and sees Enzo on the ground, no longer crying, but can visibly see the trails of previous tears from a quick glance at his cheeks.

"Are you okay, ragazzino?"

Enzo looks up, sniffles once, and shakes his head.

The man is accompanied by two other men, who are taller and more built than him and a little boy. "Do you want to talk about it?"

Enzo, seeing the little boy who stares at Enzo with amazement, smiles at Enzo, who smiles back. After seeing the little boy, Enzo nods his head.

The man looks at one of his men and nods once. One of the men breaks away from the side of the man and crouches down to help Enzo to his feet. Once he is standing, Enzo stands next to the man, who leads him down half a block and into a restaurant at the corner of the block, right where Luca is selling bonds. Enzo avoids eye contact with him, but Luca watches in shock as he sees Enzo Mazzante, a poor boy from a poverty-stricken family, walk into a restaurant with one of the most feared men in Sicily, Godfather Giuseppe Russo.

Enzo swiftly became close with his newly found friend, which the don insisted that Enzo called him Uncle Russo.

Enzo also became very close with his son, Marco, who is only one year younger than Enzo; and they quickly formed a great friendship, seeing each other every day. The don quickly caught onto Enzo's financial situation and would give Enzo twenty dollars a day to take home to his family. After a few months of bringing home money every day, Ms. Giambruno demanded to know from Enzo where the money was coming from. Enzo quickly said the money came from Uncle Russo. Ms. Giambruno knew exactly who Enzo was referring to.

"I don't want you going to him anymore. He's a bad man."

Of course, Enzo didn't believe his mother, and quite frankly, he didn't care. He was making money to provide for his family. Enzo was livid when he heard what his mother said about Uncle Russo. "He's paying for us to put food on the table. You should be grateful."

His mother snapped and walked up to her son, slapping him harshly across the cheek. "Don't you ever talk back to me like that."

Enzo turned away from his mother, holding his now reddened cheek. Tears start falling down his face. He doesn't turn to face his mother. He gets up and runs out of his home, neither his mother nor his siblings stopping him. He was eleven years old. He didn't come back.

He began living with his Uncle Russo, who became a father to him, and Marco a brother. From the age of eleven until eighteen, he lived with Uncle Russo, eventually going into business with him through selling furniture as a gift for his eighteenth birthday. While setting up a shop in the city, he ran into a man who was selling fruits out of his shop across the street from him, whom he recognized immediately as Luca Ricci, his childhood friend. Immediately, he walked over to Luca and gave him a handshake. Luca looked him up and down and let go of his hand quickly. Enzo was confused but remembered their last encounter all those years ago.

"I just wanted to say my apologies for the bonds and leaving you alone on that corner."

Luca didn't respond. He grunted and went back to selling his fruit. After a few customers came and went, Luca finally turned to speak to Enzo. "It's a good thing you left when you did."

Enzo gives Luca a look, which caught Luca off guard for a moment. "Why is that?"

"Two days later, the Carabinieri came into my father's shop and took everything from him. They then sent him to jail, where he remains to this day."

Enzo was shocked. Maybe Mr. Ricci's greed finally got the best of him. "What happened?"

"The war bonds we were selling by the hundreds every week were counterfeit. My father was able to replicate the design of the bond, and he printed them out by the thousands. He ended up getting caught, and he could've walked. All he had to do was say his name, but he didn't."

Enzo is now drowning in confusion, looking at Luca with a look of pure perplexity. "Whose name are you talking about?"

Luca just grunted and shrugged. "Ask your Uncle Russo. That's where most of the money went to when the week was done. He worked for him."

Enzo was floored. He looked at Luca, but before he could speak, Luca had turned around and left. Enzo was flooding with emotions.

Everything made sense now. That's why he didn't let him buy the bonds. That's why he was greedy. That's why he was a recluse. Enzo sat down on the sidewalk and began to cry as the day's brightly lit sun beat down on his miserable neck.

His tears didn't last long as his workers had finished setting up the store, which eventually became a front after two years of legitimate business.

After those two years, Enzo decided to leave, buying a one-way ticket to America. Somehow, he managed to convince Marco to come with him, leaving his father without an heir to the Palermo throne of power.

Marco didn't care much for that anyways.

Together, they landed in the port of Baltimore in 1924, and by 1925, they were in Philadelphia, where they continued their professional criminal careers. They found their niche in bootlegging; and by 1929, they were multimillionaires, both becoming made before the age of twenty-five. From there, Enzo made his way up the ranks, becoming underboss to the Sicilian crime syndicate in Philly.

Unlike Marco, Enzo loved power, fame, and fortune. By the time he was thirty, he had become the boss of Philly. Ever since then, he married his beautiful wife, Stella, and had a baby boy, Giacomo Giambruno; but everyone called him by his English-spelled name, Jamey. After ten years of having only one child and a horrible tragedy that befell young Giacomo's friend, the Giambruno family proudly adopted three young Irish children: Finley, Ronan, and Donald McCullough.

XII

First Sight

Donnie wakes up a few hours later around eight thirty in the morning and, without eating breakfast, immediately hops in a car with Enzo and drives to Benjamin Franklin University Hospital on South Eleventh Street and walks into the waiting room. They walk up to the receptionist desk; but Donnie's eyes veer and meet with the sight of a nurse, a young girl about twenty-two with stunning red hair and a beautiful smile with heart-piercing blue eyes—a blue so vibrant, it reminds Donnie of the oceans. Their eyes lock, and in that moment, it is love at first sight for Donnie.

She is dressed in standard medical scrubs, but even in those, Donnie can't take his eyes off her. She is gorgeous. Enzo notices where Donnie's eyes are and taps him happily on the shoulder a few times. She stands up from her chair, and just as she is fully arisen, the receptionist emerges from a back room and sits down at the desk. "Kiara, Dr. Carcetti wants to see you."

Immediately, Enzo interjects proudly. "What good timing? We're here to see Dr. Carcetti too. My son here broke his wrist. Terrible accident at the bar. Guy got too drunk and almost killed the bartender. Donnie saved his life. My boy's a hero."

Donnie's view shifts from Kiara to Enzo, who winks at Donnie with a chuckle. Donnie's face erupts with an appreciative smile, and his view shifts back to the lovely Kiara. When Donnie is looking at

65

her, his mind doesn't even think about his wrist. His eyes are dead-locked on Kiara's and hers on Donnie's. In that moment, all Donnie can do is mumble and smile like a drunken idiot. All Kiara is think-ing about is how adorable the young Donnie looks, even though he sounded like an idiot.

Her eyes lock with Donnie's, feeling his unfaltering, powerful gaze. After a few minutes, Donnie is still looking at Kiara, not drool-ing, but Kiara could see Donnie doing things to her in his head. Kiara places the papers down and looks back at Donnie with a smirky smile. "Can I help you with anything, sir?"

Donnie mumbles incoherent words but composes himself after a few seconds. "My apologies, miss. My name is Donnie McCullough. May I ask what yours is?"

Through a stifling smile, Kiara responds with a voice compa-rable to an angel. "Kiara. Kiara Maffezzoli. My friends call me Kay."

Donnie sticks his hand out, and Kiara shakes his outstretched hand, Donnie blown away by the eloquent, velvety softness of her skin. "Pleased to meet you, Kay."

As Donnie pulls his hand away, Kiara looks at Donnie's other wrist, limply hanging at the joint.

"I heard your dad say that you broke saving a bartender's life. Is that really what happened?"

Donnie's face blushes up immediately. "Nah, I wasn't saving no one. Swung awkwardly on one of my punches and broke my wrist."

Kiara nods slowly, as if she still doesn't believe what Donnie says but accepts it anyways. "Did you start the fight?"

"No, but I sure as hell finished it."

Kiara chuckles at Donnie's remark, her smile growing slightly, which makes Donnie even more giddy than before. Just then, the receptionist motions for Donnie, Enzo, and Kiara to go to Dr. Carcetti's office. The pair laughs for a few moments about Donnie's "fight," and by the time they finish their laughter, they reach Dr. Carcetti's office.

They walk in, but since Donnie and Enzo are there, Doc asks Kiara to leave and to return later. She agrees, but Donnie asks her for her number before she leaves. Kiara smirks at Donnie but quickly jots down her number on a piece of paper and slips it into Donnie's pocket before leaving the office. Donnie couldn't contain his smile after that.

Dr. Joseph "Doc" Carcetti sends Kiara out, just as Donnie gets her number. Donnie walks over to a chair next to Enzo, his smile stretching from cheek to cheek. After sticking the little piece of paper in his pocket, he sits down as Enzo starts talking to Dr. Carcetti. "How's it been, Joe?"

The doc sits in his chair and sighs loudly in an abrasive manner. "Just...fuckin' perfect. I've been swarmed with patients recently, especially gunshot victims."

Then, the tension breaks slightly as Doc leans back in his chair. "Hopefully none of them can be traced back to you, Uncle E!"

Doc playfully jabs at his Uncle Enzo, who playfully jabs back.

"But other than that, I'm stuck in my office. What do you need?"

"Need you to fix Donnie's arm. Normally, I would just wait like any other person, but I got an important meeting in half an hour and wanna be there on time."

Doc stands up and walks over to Donnie's arm, feeling it up lightly to not further any injury.

"The good type or bad type of meeting?"

"Good."

Doc nods slowly as his face makes a look, his fingers moving back and forth over a certain area above the wrist to feel for a fracture.

"Somebody get whacked?"

"Yeah. Books. Shot up in the northeast. Was supposed to be a hit on Mick or Nicky, but they accidentally hit Books instead."

"Jesus."

Finally, Doc nods and walks away from Donnie, opening a cabinet full of medical supplies. After a few minutes of rummaging around, he pulls out a soft cast and wraps it around Donnie's wrist, tightening the straps.

"Keep that on for four weeks and take acetaminophen if it starts to hurt. Anything else, Uncle E?"

"Nope. All good now. Thanks, Joey. I'll hopefully not see you soon!"

Enzo and Doc start playfully jabbing each other as Donnie and Enzo wave goodbye and leave, en route to their meeting, ready to avenge Book's death.

XIII

The Rat

As soon as Donnie and Enzo walk inside, the whole bar goes silent. Since it's early in the morning, there are only four guys there: Sals, Sally Two, their informant, and the bartender, who was there since about seven to clean up the bar.

Their informant is Juliano "Figs" Paduli. Figs had a troubled past as a kid, bouncing from foster home to foster home until he landed himself amongst the wise guys in Fishtown. The only and eldest boy of three children, his father abandoned his mother and twin sisters when they were barely six months old.

Shortly after that, his mother attempted to hang herself in the attic. Figs walked in on his mother hanging limply from the ceiling and ran to get the neighbors, who called the ambulance. They got her down and she lived, but not before scarring Figs. Due to her rapidly declining mental health, CPS took her children away, sending them to different foster homes, further ripping the family apart. Mrs. Paduli was out of the hospital staying with a friend when she heard that they had taken her children away.

That was the final string. Finding a gun in her friend's apartment, she swiftly put a bullet through her head not even two days after hearing the news.

Figs was five years old.

For the next decade, he would bounce from foster home to foster home. He had a variety of foster parents, from abusive to loving to negligent to caring. Regardless, he hated living in foster homes, and at the age of fifteen, he ran away from home in the cold morning hours of early January 1950.

After getting about five or six blocks away, at around one in the morning, he ran into a man, about five foot eight and 240 pounds, dressed in a long-sleeved button-down and khakis, covered in a mysterious liquid running down his shirt, presumably alcohol. The man turned and faced the scared teenager, his face covered in a combined look of sadness and astonishment. That man was Salvatore "Sals" Andresano. "You okay, figlio? What are you doing out so late?"

"I'm running away."

The man steps back and looks at the boy in amazement, sticking a cigar in his mouth during the process.

"Running away? Now, why would you do that, figlio? Don't you love your parents? Don't your parents love—"

"They aren't my parents."

Figs's cutting off Sals shocks him even more. If Figs had known who he was talking to, he surely wouldn't have cut off Sals. If Sals had taken offense to Figs's interruption, Figs would've had his tongue cut out of his mouth within moments. Sals smirked happily at Figs after interrupting him. It was ballsy. Sals admired that. "Whaddaya mean they aren't your parents?"

"They're my foster parents."

"What happened to your real ones?"

"My father abandoned me, and my mother killed herself."

Sals felt horrible for asking the question. He looked away from Figs for a moment; and when he looked back, Figs was staring at the concrete, crying softly.

"Hey, it's all right, figlio. Say…what's your name?"

Figs wiped his face, tear stains spreading on his cheeks and under his eyes. "Juliano Paduli."

"Paduli, you say? Sicilian?"

He nodded a few times before looking at Sals, whose interest was piqued toward the small teenager.

"Both of my parents were born in Pozzallo."

Sals's face lit up with joy, a smile quickly stretching from ear to ear. "No fuckin' shit. I was born in Pozzallo. I moved here when I was a baby. Name's Sals. Pleased to meet you, Juliano."

As Figs reached for Sals outstretched hand and shook it, for the first time in nearly a decade, he smiled. Sals pulled Figs up so that he was standing and no longer sitting on the cold concrete sidewalk outside of the bustling bar on the corner of East Girard. Sals brought him inside the bar and warmed him up a little bit and they talked for hours, but to Figs, it felt like forever.

When talking to Sals, he felt at ease; and after that night, he went under Sals wing, learning the ropes of being a wise guy. About a week after running away, he started living with Sals, who treated him as a son. Figs was all Sals had to look forward to since he hadn't been married up to that point. Having Figs under him as a pupil gave Sals purpose. It made him happy. For the next decade and more, Sals became one hell of a wise guy, eventually getting his button and becoming made, officially becoming part of Giambruno crime family.

Shortly after the Mazzante family brought down the former Mahony captain's drug operation, Figs was sent to infiltrate the Mazzante organization, acting as a double agent for the Giambruno family, primarily to make sure that no one put any contracts on members of the Giambruno family. This is where Enzo found out about the three men that Mick and Nicky clipped.

They were apparently planning on putting a hit out on Enzo as he was the only other family in Philadelphia that Angelo had to deal with since he had either taken or iced all other competition in the city.

After Books got whacked, Figs decided to meet with Enzo, Donnie, Sally Two, and Sals.

When Figs walks into Mikey's bar, he sees Sals for the first time in years, giving him a large hug and smiling widely.

"Juli! How've you been, figlio?"

"Been good, Sals. Missed seeing you around here."

Figs places a hand on Sals's shoulder, tapping it twice before receiving a kiss on each cheek from Sals. Just after that, Donnie and Enzo walk in, and everyone takes a few minutes to greet each other before sitting down at a booth in the corner of the bar. Enzo is on edge and very curious of what Figs will say since he had an inside in the Mazzante organization.

"Okay, whaddaya got for me?"

"Well, it was the Mazzantes that hit Books. It was two guys, some new associate that's been there for a few months. I never got his name. The other was Mazzante's own son, Carlo. He wanted to clip Mick or Nicky, so he's willing to meet and discuss and apologize as Books was clipped."

Enzo sits back in the booth, peering around outside of the bar.

"Bullshit. How the fuck did they find out it was Mick and Nicky? There were three guys, and all three got shot to hell. I'm trying to figure out who saw them."

The whole table goes silent. Donnie can see that Enzo begins to think what everyone else is thinking but are too scared to say it. Finally, after a few minutes, Sals speaks his mind. "Maybe…maybe we got a rat?"

Donnie watched Enzo purse his lips and sigh heavily. After another minute of silence, he nods in agreement. "Maybe, Sals. Maybe. That's the only thing that makes sense. Did'ya hear about any witnesses, Figs?"

Figs shakes his head quickly and wipes his brow of sweat as the morning sun begins to peek through the bar window.

"No. It was three in the morning. The only people who would be out there that late would be the dope fiends, and they're too high to recognize anything."

Enzo nods a few times before pulling out a cigar, lighting it and taking a few puffs before placing it on an ashtray.

"Okay. Donnie, I need you and Sals to look for people who could've ratted on us. Get Maxo to help you too. I'll set up the meeting with Carlo. Figs, you keep an ear out for us. Thanks a lot. See you later, gentlemen."

Enzo stands up, and everyone follows suit, taking a few minutes to say their goodbyes before departing Mikey's one by one. After a minute, Donnie and Enzo are the only two people left in the bar with the exception of the bartender, who is wiping the bar down. Just as they are about to get into the car, Enzo grabs Donnie's arm harshly and pulls him close, his lips nearly touching Donnie's ear.

"Keep an eye on Figs. He's acting fidgety. Can you drive with this shit on?"

Enzo makes a slight motion toward Donnie's soft cast, which Donnie brushes away.

"I'll be fine. I'll follow him to where he's headed."

Enzo nods and kisses both of Donnie's cheeks before walking to another car behind Donnie's, driving home from the bar. Donnie hops in his car, catching up with Figs at a red light. Donnie is directly behind him, which is not how you want to tail someone. Once it turns green, Donnie waits a few moments before driving again, gaining some distance between himself and Figs. They drive down Girard Avenue, making their way toward Broad Street.

After hopping on Broad, they head south for about two miles, making a right onto Lombard Street. From there, they drive for about a mile, turning onto Schuylkill Avenue. From there, they drive another half mile, stopping as Figs turns into a warehouse parking lot where the Giambruno family make their swag runs. From a distance, Donnie sees Figs begin conversing with the driver of an adjacent car.

For a few minutes, Donnie couldn't make out who Figs is talking to. Eventually, Figs gets out of his car and pops his trunk up, revealing what seems to be a brick of cocaine. The man in the adjacent car, at last, leaves his car, revealing his face. Donnie is floored. Donnie couldn't fuckin' believe Figs would do this.

After approaching the trunk of the car and seeing the package, Carlo Mazzante hands Figs a large yellow envelope, presumably filled with an exorbitant amount of money. After this, Figs and Carlo switch cars and drive away. After driving away, Donnie heads back to Mikey's Bar, in complete disarray that Figs turned out to be the rat after all.

XIV

Signification of Acceptance

That same night after finding out that Figs has turned on them, Donnie has a date planned for him and Kiara. He is looking forward to it but needs to take care of business first. That's how being a wise guy works. Business first, everything else second.

After seeing Figs turn and pull a cocaine deal on them, which Enzo strictly forbids in his family, Donnie goes back to Mikey's to see if any of the guys will be there; but since it is only a little after one in the afternoon, the bar is empty. Still in shock, Donnie heads home, where Pops is, awaiting his news on Figs. Stella isn't home; so Donnie walks in on Enzo in his office, with Maxo Salucci and Sals Andresano, giving them the plan on figuring out who the rat is. After waiting a few seconds for them to look up, Donnie blurts it out. "It's Figs."

The whole room stops, all of them making movements to face Donnie as he stands at the entrance of the door, his body relieved for revealing the rat; but his face disturbed by Sals's sudden interjection.

"What the fuck did you just say?"

Sals starts walking slowly toward Donnie, his face engulfed with anger.

"Figs is the rat, Sals. I just fuckin' saw him do a coke deal with Carlo Mazzante."

Sals's teeth are clenched together in anger. Donnie knows Sals sees Figs as a son, just as Enzo sees Donnie as his.

That's why everyone calls him Figs. Sals called him figlio the first few times they spoke, so everyone ended up calling him Figs.

Sals walks up to Donnie, their faces now inches apart. Sals's teeth are bared, looking like he is going to rip Donnie's face off. "You're fuckin' lying. Figs wouldn't do—"

"Pops had me tail him, Sals."

Sals doesn't like that Donnie cut him off. Even in his age, Sals is quick. Like lightning, Sals grabs Donnie's shirt collar, rears back, and socks him right across the nose.

"Oh! Fuck! You son of a bitch! You…fuckin' asshole!"

Sals's punch felt like a freight train on Donnie's nose. Donnie's face absorbs the hit as he falls to the floor in writhing pain. After staring down at Donnie for a few moments, Sals shoots a look of pain at Enzo.

"Is it true?"

Somberly, Enzo nods once, his face emotionless, even while looking at Donnie on the floor, his nose slowly starting to bleed. Sals breaks down. He falls to his knees and starts sobbing audibly in short spurts. Pops taps Maxo on the shoulder and motions for him to pick Sals up, who is now nearly prostrated on the floor. Maxo slowly walks over and picks Sals up by the arms, who sniffles loudly before wiping his tears away.

"I'm sorry, Sals."

Sals nods once as a tear rolls down his face, which he quickly wipes away. He looks at Enzo and nods once more, this time with a stoic face, signifying his acceptance of the reality of the situation, as well as accepting to do what needs to be done.

During all of this, Donnie is still on the floor, now bleeding a waterfall of blood out of his nose. "Hey Pops, could you toss me a fuckin' towel or a napkin or something. Jesus, it's everywhere."

Maxo pulls a handkerchief out of his jacket pocket and tosses it to Donnie, who quickly put it on his nose to stop the bleeding.

"Hey… I'm sorry, Donnie. I didn't mean to. I thought you were fuckin' with me. I'm really sorry, Donnie."

Sals starts breaking down bad again. He starts crying again as Maxo just stands there and pats his shoulder till his tears calmed down.

"Why don't you go home, calm yourself down a little, Sals? Come back tonight. We'll talk then."

Sals nods a few times and leaves the room, apologizing to Donnie once more before leaving Enzo's office entirely. After he leaves and the trio hears the front door open and close, Enzo calls Donnie and Maxo close to his desk.

"All right. Since we don't have to worry about finding the rat, let's take care of this meeting. Maxo's will take the lead, but I don't want him to go alone. So you go with him, Donnie. We need to meet in a place, preferably outside the city. Somewhere safe. Somewhere neutral. Somewhere where they won't expect us to whack them."

After careful research, Enzo decided on Il Siciliano Villaggio, the Sicilian Village, a mom-and-pop Italian restaurant in the western suburbs of Philadelphia. Since it is neutral territory, the Mazzante family hopefully wouldn't be suspicious of the place. Enzo, of course, knows that they would have the place scouted out beforehand, which means they have to scout it out after they are there. After deciding the place, they decide the date. After careful consideration, the trio decides on the following night, August 19, at nine thirty in the evening.

Maxo will arrive with Donnie at 9:20 p.m., exactly ten minutes early. Pops will have people inside of the restaurant already, acting as bystanders. Maxo, since he wasn't there when Mick or Nicky hit the Mazzante guys or when Books got clipped, will sit down in the restaurant with Carlo and his associate. Meanwhile, out in the car, Donnie will be waiting, ready to whack whoever is at the table with Maxo, as well as anyone else still standing. Bystanders paid by Enzo will be in there, and once they see Maxo head toward the back, they're gonna duck under their table or behind their booth 'cause that's what they've been told to do.

"If there's anyone else standing after you whack them booth, shoot them too. We don't want any real witnesses."

Minus the chefs and the attendees of the meeting, there should only be about four to five people in there. The plan is that they will sit down and order their appetizer and drinks, and after ordering their entree, Maxo will get up to go to the bathroom. But instead, he will sneak out the backdoor. After that, Donnie will walk in and clip the two guys.

"Donnie, Maxo will sit at the center table, so you don't even have to enter the joint. Just shoot them through the fuckin' front window. Only enter if you aren't 100 percent sure they're dead."

After clipping them, Donnie would get in the car driven by Sals and pull up to an alleyway, which leads to the back exit to pick up Maxo; and they'd be gone, dumping the pieces before heading home for the night.

In and out. Twenty minutes tops.

Maxo and Donnie nod as Enzo approves of the plan and would introduce it to Angelo, who would inform his son and associate of the meeting.

"I'll keep you posted if the meeting gets the okay or not. Till then, it's on."

After finalizing and going through the minute details of the meeting, Maxo and Donnie leave Enzo's office, with Maxo leaving the house entirely. In the meantime, Donnie has a date to get ready for. He's taking Kiara to dinner and a show at Baldassarri, a black-tie nightclub about six blocks east of Broad Street on South Street.

Baldassarri is always thriving with bosses, capos, wise guys, and associates from mobs all over the city; and tonight, Donnie will be given a special shout-out by famous comedian Davey Balter, as Enzo knew Davey through business deals of years past.

David Balter is born to Jewish parents in 1934 in West Philadelphia. His parents are hard workers and always provide Davey with everything he needs: food, clothes, money, even a car once he was able to drive. After graduating high school, Davy joins the Army and serves in the Korean War for two years.

After coming back home, he decides, much to his father's dismay, that he wants to become a comedian, as he always enjoys making people laugh, even if it is at himself. Davey struggles, both financially and emotionally, for the first few years of his career until he is able to land a spot for nighttime comedian at Baldassarri. At the young age of twenty-five and being Philly born and raised, he loves the crowd and how supportive they are. For the first half hour of his show, Davey has the crowd keeled over in laughter. Jokingly, Davey starts making comedic jabs about the mob presence in the city.

"Okay, so one day, a mob boss decides he wants to test one of his captains to see if he has what it takes to lead the business, as the boss is becoming frail, weak, and old.

"'Tony,' he asks. 'If you received stolen money, and you were looking for a place to hide it, where would you stash it so the cops could never get it?'

"Tony thinks for a moment, then says, 'I'd put it in a casino.'

"Delighted, the mob boss exclaims, 'Magnificent answer! How did you know to launder your money through the casino?'

"'Well,' Tony says, 'at school, we learned that the Constitution protects us from police conducting unreasonable search in Caesar's.'"

Immediately, the crowd begins roaring with laughter but most noticeably is a young mob boss by the name of Enzo Giambruno, boss of the family, sitting in the front row right in front of Davey. Davey has no clue who Enzo is until after the show when Enzo goes backstage to meet with the young Davey Balter.

"Mr. Balter…how's it going?"

Davey turns around and smiles at the man, who is standing there with his wife. After taking a drink of water to soothe his aching throat from the long show, Davey gladly greets his future unknown gangster friend.

"How's it going…"

"Giambruno. Enzo Giambruno and this is my wife, Stella."

"How are you doing, ma'am?"

Mrs. Giambruno reached out and shook Davey's hand lightly.

"Say, Mr. Balter, I really liked your jokes out there. I think you got a lot of talent, and I would like you to come back here again."

Davey smiles widely while taking another sip of water. "Oh, that's very gracious of you saying that you enjoy my time here, but I'd have to talk to the people here cause—"

"Ah, don't worry about it. I own the joint. Come back whenever you like. Actually, you wanna go out for drinks tonight?"

Of course, on paper, it belongs to Enzo's long-dead mother; but in actuality, it is run by Enzo and his team.

"Wait...you're serious?"

"What, you think I'm bullshitting you? Of course, I'm fuckin' serious."

Davey is blown away. He doesn't know what to say. "I'm stunned. Thank you, Mr. Giambruno."

"Call me Enzo."

"Thank you, Enzo. I can't do drinks tonight, but how about tomorrow night?"

"Tomorrow night's perfect. See ya then."

Just as Enzo and Stella were leaving the backstage, Davey kindly asked them a question. "If you don't mind me asking, Enzo, but did you have a favorite joke tonight?"

Enzo's face makes a look of contemplation as he deeply thinks about the various jokes that Davey had said that left Enzo laughing so hard, he nearly cried. After a few moments, he nods and answers the question. "The mob joke. I laughed really hard about that one. 'Unreasonable search at Caesar's'—that's a fuckin' good one."

Davey is proud that Enzo liked his joke so much. "Thanks. It took me a little bit to get it down pat. Any particular reason you liked that one the most?"

Enzo looks at Davey for a moment and lets out a little chuckle. "Sounds like something I would do."

Davey and Enzo start laughing together, with Davey thinking Enzo is joking. After the pair laugh for a minute, Enzo says his good-byes and Davey goes about his night.

Eventually, Davey finds out about Enzo's involvement in organized crime; but by then, he had helped make Davey so much money as well as give him a place and an audience he could call home that he didn't care.

Now, Davey does shows at Baldassarri's three to four times a year, with one of them being the night that Donnie and Kiara have their first date.

Once the couple arrives, Donnie has one of the many valets park his car, a 1971 Cadillac Fleetwood, about a block away from the nightclub. Donnie slips him a hundred-dollar bill from the wad of money he has in his hands. Donnie must've had at least ten thousand dollars in that wad. On date nights, tipping the help is like giving away candy on Halloween. That's how wise guys work.

Donnie has all of his money from two days ago at the card games and anything he took off Joey Slur. The night that he and Kiara are out is a Friday night, so there is a line about three blocks long to get into the club. But since Enzo owns it, all Donnie has to do is walk up to the front of the line, slip the bouncer a hundred-dollar bill, and walk right into the place. The bouncer knows Donnie already since he had been there a million times before. He just smiles brightly as Donnie slips a few bills into his front jacket pocket.

"Thanks, Donnie!"

That's all Donnie hears all night, from the bouncer to the host to the waiters to the surrounding tables. Donnie and Kiara walk from the front door up to the host stand, where there is still a line of people that leads to the door, and immediately, the host whistles loudly. And on cue, like a Broadway performer coming from behind the curtain, two waiters carry a table, placing it directly in front of the stage.

Donnie slips a buck into the host and each of the waiters' pockets before sitting down with Kiara. Donnie is talking to everyone because everyone is there tonight to see Davey. Donnie sees Vinny Ruge and his wife Emilia, a beautiful Sicilian broad from South Philly who Donnie had known for years, and Maxo Salucci and his girlfriend. He even sees Sally Two and his wife, Priscilla, who he always complained about at Mikey's. Only after Donnie and Kiara sit down is Donnie able to see the look on her face. She is blown away. Kiara looks at Donnie the way that teenagers look at their favorite celebrity. Wise guys always love that kind of look from women.

After Donnie and Kiara sit down, almost immediately, the show starts; and the crowd, who had been conversing loudly throughout the nightclub, has died down to low murmurs as the announcer comes onto the stage.

"Ladies and gentlemen, your show tonight, Davey Balter!"

The entire nightclub erupts in cheers, whistles, and applause as a tall man—about six foot one, with a slim figure dressed in a dashing all-white suit, a stylish colorful shirt unbuttoned down to the top of his chest, with a golden chain that drooped down his naked chest—walks out on stage.

"Hey, how's it going everyone? Thank you…thank you! Well, it's good to be back everyone. Good to be home. I've been in Vegas for the past month doing shows and I love it there. But there's no place like home, folks. I'll tell ya that."

More applause and cheers erupt from the crowd as Davey Balter smiles widely and begins pacing across the stage.

"Of course, I love it here, but it's always better when I get a show the same night as one of my personal friends, Donnie McCullough! Let's give him a hand, folks!"

The whole nightclub explodes with applause as Donnie looks around at the tables with Vinny Ruge, Maxo, and Sally Two, who are all raising their glasses to him and smoking their cigars.

"Amazing guy. Amazing man. Come on, stand up. Donnie McCullough, everyone!"

Donnie shoots Kiara a large smile, who shoots him one back as he stands up from his chair and turns around, waving at the audience in the nightclub. After a few seconds, he sits back down and calls one of the waiters over, who leans his ear over Donnie's mouth.

"Get me your best wine!"

Donnie slips a buck into the waiter's pocket and nods happily as he leaves, returning a few minutes later with a fine bottle of Chateau Margaux, pouring Donnie and Kiara a glass each, placing the bottle in an ice bucket at the center of the table before leaving.

The rest of the night goes off without a hitch. Donnie and Kiara talk for what feels like an eternity. After finishing their night and saying their goodbyes to the guys, Donnie walks out of the nightclub where a valet is waiting with his car.

"Did you enjoy your night?"

"Oh, it was just wonderful, Donnie. I didn't know you were so famous. I thought you worked as a bartender."

"Well, you meet a lot of interesting people as a bartender. A lot of famous people. A lot of rich people. People that pay good money."

Of course, Donnie knows that, on paper, he worked as a bartender. But in actuality, Donnie is closer to a barfly than a bartender. Donnie proceeds to lie to Kiara about how he is also in the stock market, which is why he makes so much money and not all of it is from bartending. Kiara, though she feels suspicious of the origin of his income, brushes it away. Maybe she wants to think he is lying but is thinking too dreamy of Donnie to care otherwise.

After hopping in his car, Donnie drives Kiara home to her small apartment building in South Philadelphia. After he parks the car, he gets out and walks her to her apartment, where the couple stand in her doorway, feeling the tension between each other grow stronger and stronger.

"Would you like a drink?" Kiara's angelic voice rumbles in Donnie's ears for a moment before he politely declines.

"I would love to, but I'm not trying to wreck my car heading home tonight."

"Who said anything about you heading home tonight?"

Donnie stops for a moment and calmly walks into her apartment as she walks into her kitchen area, turning on the lights and delving into the liquor cabinet.

"What's your poison?"

"Whiskey."

"You really are an Irishman."

Donnie nervously chuckles as Kiara walks over to him, sitting down on the couch. She politely hands him a glass, filled about halfway with whiskey, as she sits down on the across from him. After sitting down, both Donnie and Kiara raised their glasses simultaneously.

"Salud!"

Both of them down their glasses, Donnie sighing happily as Kiara stands up, grabs Donnie's glass, and places them in the sink. As she walks back toward the couch, she walks up behind Donnie, wrapping her forearms around his upper body, her lips ever so slightly touching his neck. Her lips move around his neck, her hair drooping over his cheeks. In one swift motion, Donnie pulls her over the back of the couch, their lips meeting as she softly lands on top of him. In seconds, their impassioned kiss becomes more longing, more tender, and more amorous.

Slowly, Donnie creeps his hand up the bottom of her skirt, his hand meeting her inner thigh. Her hands slowly begin to unbutton his shirt, one by one, as he slips off his jacket, her hands creeping up his stomach and chest with her fingers slowly clutching his large golden chain. Then, in a flash, they are both nearly nude in Kiara's living room, wrapped up in their own salacious fantasy.

XV

Night to Remember

Donnie hasn't slept that well since before the war. Maybe it was the alcohol, but regardless, Donnie slept like a baby. He wakes up at three o'clock in the afternoon and would've slept later before he realizes what day it is. Donnie shoots up off the covers and gets dressed as quick as he can. Rushing, he races out of the bedroom as Kiara is sitting on her couch watching TV.

"Going somewhere?"

"Yeah, overslept. Gotta be at Mikey's by four for work."

"Oh…okay. Well, stay safe. Take a coffee for the road."

Kiara walks into her kitchen and grabs a mug filled to the brim with black coffee, handing it to Donnie as he makes his way toward the door.

"I'll be busy tonight. I'll call you when I can."

Donnie leads in and gives her a quick peck on the lips before leaving her apartment building.

Donnie gets to Mikey's by four thirty and goes right down to the basement, where Maxo Salucci and Sals are waiting for Donnie, getting ready for tonight's hit.

There is a table with weapons of all varieties laid out on it. It looks like the remnants of a military armory. There are pistols, revolvers, rifles, machine guns, shotguns, all with or without suppressor capability, and even hand grenades and Molotov cocktails. A wise-guy's paradise.

Donnie's personal choice is his revolver, chambered-in .38, with a Colt .45 as a backup piece. There are pussy guns that are chambered-in .32, which is practically the same as a .38 but with less kickback. Most of the time, they're carried by women as defense pieces, thus why they call them pussy guns. Regardless, every hit is something different.

If you want noise, you use a .45. If you want to rip through multiple people, you use a shotgun, a machine gun, or both. If you want it to be quick, quiet, and clean, you'd use a .38, which is what most guys end up using.

For a few hours, the trio goes through their guns, sorting through what they need and what they don't. Since they don't want to burn the place down or blow it up, they put away the Molotovs and grenades. They put away the machine guns but keep out the shotgun.

After a few minutes, Donnie decides on a pump-action shotgun, with his signature piece as a backup. Donnie cuts the barrel down about eight inches and chops the stock off, turning it into a makeshift sawn-off. Maxo Salucci decides to carry a Colt .45 on his backside, though most likely he'll get patted down, and as an if-all-hell-breaks-loose last resort, Sals will be inside the car with a .38.

Around eight thirty in the evening, the guys start getting ready to leave. Maxo puts on soft body armor under his dress shirt just in case things go south inside the restaurant before Donnie has time to react. They clean their guns, run one last check on them, and then get in the car, heading en route to The Sicilian Village by 8:50 p.m., arriving there by 9:20 p.m. on the dot. Ten minutes early. Just as Enzo wants.

Maxo gets out of the car and walks into the restaurant, the bright neon sign flashing Il Siciliano Villaggio, bouncing off the contours of his deep Sicilian mug. The small restaurant has seven tables laid out in honeycomb fashion around the restaurant, with the six tables surrounding one table in the center, where Maxo, Carlo, and his associate are meeting. Donnie sits in the car, waiting for Maxo to remove himself from the chair and "walk to the bathroom." Other than the three people for the meeting, there were about seven other people there and two chefs.

Maxo sits down at the table and waits for Carlo and his associate to show up. By 9:25 p.m., a taxicab pulls up to the front of the restaurant, dropping off two men dressed in suits and gold chains around their necks and wrists. One of them has brown hair lazily combed backward that Donnie didn't recognize, who must be Carlo's associate. The other man has jet-black hair, slicked back and as shiny as a new set of rims, who Donnie recognizes immediately as Carlo Mazzante.

He watches as both of them enter the restaurant, walking over to the table where Maxo is. Maxo sees this and stands up, shaking both of their hands accordingly. Though Donnie can't hear anything, Carlo motions to his associate, who pats down Maxo, pulling a Colt .45 from the small of his back, placing it in his inner jacket pocket.

From there, Maxo, Carlo, and his man order wine and caprese as their appetizers, as Donnie watches from the safety of the car window, the little voice in the back of his head running him paranoid that things are going to go south. Donnie rechecks, double-checks, and triple checks his guns, occupying his mind to make sure he doesn't go crazy.

That passes the time for about twenty minutes. When Donnie looks up, their entrees are just coming to the table. Any second now. Donnie sits motionless in the car, waiting for Maxo to get up. He watches as Maxo takes a few bites of his food and slides his chair back, standing up and excusing himself from the room to take a bathroom break. By the time he stands up, Donnie is out of the car and making his way to the restaurant front and stares inside for a moment. As he approaches the storefront, he looks at the table where Carlo is and his heart stops.

He miscalculated the distance.

With the shotgun, the distance is too far. He would hit them, but they wouldn't die from it. Donnie has two to three shots max to make sure they are gone for good. Donnie has to go inside. He has no choice.

Donnie had been dressed in a suit and a trench coat that went all the way down to his ankles, so he doesn't have to worry about them seeing the shotgun, whose length is now a foot and a half long, compared to the original length of thirty-two inches. With reluctant fear, Donnie props the collar of his coat up against his neck and walks inside Il Siciliano Villaggio.

As he walks in, Donnie realizes that the table that Carlo is at isn't in the center of the restaurant but about ten to fifteen feet further back than initially anticipated. Then, he looks at the table setup, and Carlo isn't at the center table but at the back one.

Maxo sat at the wrong fuckin' table!

Donnie is livid but keeps his cool and walks up to the counter, where a plate of fresh cannoli is sitting behind a glass barrier. Donnie is about ten feet to the right of the table. Perfect distance. Donnie slowly reaches down and wraps my hand around the stock of the gun. Just then, one of the chefs walks up to the counter.

"Would you like anything, sir?"

"Yeah, get me a plate of those cannoli."

Donnie slides the chef a twenty-dollar bill, who sticks it right into his pocket and walks into the back to prepare the food. Donnie has to clip them now. As soon as the chef walks into the kitchen through a pair of swinging metal doors, Donnie goes to business.

In one motion, Donnie spins on his heel and whips the shotgun out from under his coat, firing from his hip. The table isn't even paying attention to Donnie, as when he looks, both men have their faces down, eating their pastas and their bruschetta.

The first shot Donnie fires hits the associate.

Since he is close, the pellets don't spread much. The shot hits him square in the upper body, ripping into his chest, neck, and mouth, as his lower face explodes like a water balloon. Blood pours swiftly out of the gaping hole in his neck where his throat was, his head nearly upside down as it hangs backward over the top of the chair.

By that time, Carlo had seen, heard, and felt the shot hitting his associate. He looks up from his food, a little piece of mozzarella and tomato stuck to his cheek with a look of incredulous fear spread across his face. Donnie takes a half a second to look at him and pump another shell in before firing his second shot.

The pellets hit Carlo in the lower section of his torso, ripping apart his stomach and damaging various other vital organs. A hole even larger than the associate's appears seemingly from nowhere, blood spilling like thick gravy from the wound. After being hit, Carlo lets out a scream of pain, a scream so bloodcurdling, Donnie still hears his voice to this day.

His scream only lasts a second.

By the time Carlo lets out his cry, Donnie walks up to him and sticks the barrel into the roof of his mouth, pulling the trigger and watching his head erupt like confetti on New Year's Eve. After that, Donnie pulls out his .38 and looks around the restaurant to see if anyone is still watching.

Seeing everyone tucked fearfully under their table, hiding themselves, Donnie is about to sprint out of the restaurant, grabbing a few cannoli and Maxo's gun from the jacket pocket of the associate, now covered in his blood. With the adrenaline pumping through his veins, Donnie races out the back door and looks down the alleyway, seeing Maxo pop the door to the car open and shout at him.

"Get in the fuckin' car!"

Donnie begins to sprint even faster, hopping in the car, which speeds away before Maxo can fully shut the door. After a few seconds of driving, Donnie drops Maxo's gun and calms down slightly. Then in a pinch, the anger comes back.

"Are you fuckin' kidding me? Are you fuckin' kidding me?!" Donnie snaps and starts smacking Maxo across the body.

"The fuck are you hitting me for?"

"The fuck am I hitting you for? You sat at the wrong fuckin' table! Pops said center table. You sat at the one in the fuckin' back! You're lucky they didn't see you leave! Jesus Christ, use your head sometimes!"

After Donnie rips into him, his body slumps down. He feels bad. Maxo is embarrassed too. Maxo is about ten years Donnie's elder and a made man, so Donnie never should've touched him at all, but Maxo knew he fucked up and he felt like shit about it. Still, Donnie felt bad for ripping into him.

"Just use your head, Maxy."

After that, Donnie wipes his hands with a handkerchief, which is covered in the blood of the associate, and grabs Maxo's .45 with it, wrapping it in the cloth and placing it on the floor. The trio drives for about twenty minutes and dumps the pieces, dropping Maxo's .45 and the sawn-off into the Schuylkill River. While pulling out the shotgun, Donnie reaches into the wrong pocket and grabs the cannoli that he put there from The Sicilian Village before grabbing the shotgun.

Donnie looks back and forth between the gun and the cannoli, ultimately tossing the piece into the river before taking a large bite of the cannoli. Maxo watches Donnie contemplate his decision, and after his piece is in the water, Maxo looks at him and starts chuckling, which grows harder and louder each time he takes a breath. After a minute or two of listening to him laugh, Donnie finally breaks. "All right, the fuck's so funny?"

Maxo takes a second to calm himself down before looking at Donnie with a big smile on his face. "What you did there. It was just like the movie."

Realizing what Maxo meant, Donnie starts laughing with Maxo, both men feeding off each other's laughter, growing louder and louder.

"Get the fuck in the car."

They are both laughing as they get in the car when Sals asks them what is going on, and after explaining to him, all three of the guys are pissing themselves laughing. It just gets funnier and funnier each time they say it.

XVI

Fort Knox

Kiara called Donnie three times that night. Enzo doesn't even tell him till the next day. Donnie always sleeps in after a hit. Claims it helps with the demons. Donnie walks into the kitchen; and Enzo is sitting at the table, drinking coffee and reading the papers, with Stella cooking eggs and bacon at the stove.

"Hey, your girlfriend called."

"Who?"

"Kiara, your girlfriend. Called ya three times last night. I didn't even pick up the phone till the third time, and once I did, she asked if Donnie was there. I said he was out and that he'd call back in the morning. Figured I'd let you know."

Donnie shrugs and walks over to the phone and dials her number, the sound of the phone rings hitting his ear before being picked up after a few seconds.

"Hello?"

"Hey, Kay. It's Donnie. Sorry about last night. I was bogged down with work. Pops told me to call you back. What's up?"

"Oh, I just wanted to call and ask if you wanted to go out again sometime soon. I really enjoyed going out with you and was wondering if you wanted to do something more casual."

Donnie is talking up a storm, trying to do anything to avoid her bringing up why he didn't call her last night. Luckily, when Kiara tells him that she wants to see him again, Donnie knows she wouldn't bring it up. The couple start talking about restaurants and places to go, and the one place she brings up an old Italian restaurant she hadn't been to since she was a kid.

This restaurant is, of course, The Sicilian Village. Donnie is eating his breakfast while talking to Kiara and nearly chokes it down when she brings up her restaurant of choice. She starts blabbering about how she went there a lot as a kid and that the owners probably still know her or some bullshit. After clearing his throat, now breathing properly, Donnie wants to explain to her but he can't. All he can think about is the papers.

"Did you get the paper yet?"

Donnie can feel her voice recoil in confusion.

"Um…no. Well, maybe. I haven't checked."

"Go read the paper, Kay."

Donnie hears Kiara place the phone down, the line staying silent while she walks over to her doorstep, opens the door, and grabs the paper. Right there on the front page is a black-and-white still photo of Carlo Mazzante and his associate, slumped over the table, blood splattered across the restaurant floor and walls magnificently. Donnie hears a yelp break the calm silence and then a loud noise of something slamming into the floor. When Kiara walks back over to the phone, Donnie can feel her voice again, this time shaky with shock, "What happened? Oh my god. That happened at The Sicilian Village?"

"Something bad, Kay. Two guys got shot in the restaurant. Must've been a gang hit or something."

"Oh my god. That's terrible."

Donnie remains silent on his whereabouts last night. Maybe Kiara knows. Maybe she doesn't. Maybe she doesn't care. Who knows? All Donnie remembers is Kiara's childish chuckle pierce through the silence of the phone, with nervous laughs following the chuckles. "I guess we won't be going there for dinner tonight."

Her quick remark makes Donnie laugh too. Laughter always helps a stressful situation. After a few minutes of laughing, Donnie calms down, and Kiara does too.

"Don't worry about it. I know just the place. How's seven tomorrow sound to you?"

"Sounds perfect, Donnie."

"All right. I'll see ya then, gorgeous."

After Donnie says that, Kiara places the phone on the receiver, ending the call. Just as it ends, her smile can hardly be contained. Her body is bursting with joy, only being released through girly shrieks and delightful stomping, like a child who has just received a favorite toy on Christmas.

Donnie has a fantastic night planned out for them. They are gonna stop by Bruno's for sandwiches and then drive to the edge of the Delaware River and eat their sandwiches under the crystal-clear night sky.

First stop is Bruno's. If Donnie gets Bruno's approval, he knows she's the one, but first, he has to pick her up. Donnie drives to her place in his '71 Cadillac, which he had freshly washed and waxed that day. He drives up to her place, and the car must've looked like a piece of the sun had fallen onto the streets of South Philly. The sun is just beginning to set behind the buildings but is still bouncing impressively off the freshly waxed exterior of the car. He waits for her to come down, watching her walk out of her apartment building and hop in his car.

"Hey, gorgeous."

"Hey, Donnie."

He leans over and gives a quick peck on the cheek before starting the car and heading back to Fishtown. Within twenty minutes, they are parked outside of Bruno's. It is about seven o'clock, and the sky is turning from a pinkish hue to a dark purple, as the Monday night sky begins to show off its starriness. Donnie walks up to the counter with a big smile on his face, as he looks at the old Italian man who smiles right back. "Aye, Bruno!"

"Donnie! How've you been?" Bruno reaches over the counter and shakes Donnie's hand, as both of their smiles grow bigger. After shaking, Bruno steps back and turns toward Kiara, looking her top to bottom and back again. "And who's this?"

"Bruno, this is Kiara Maffezzoli, my girlfriend. Kiara, Bruno Kline."

"Ah...nice to meet you, Kiara. Donnie sure picked a good-looking one."

Donnie sees Kiara blush a little as Bruno compliments her.

"All righty then. What can I get you two lovebirds?"

Donnie motions toward Kiara to go first as she leans to look at the board that holds the menu items.

"Capicola and salami with lettuce, tomato, onions, and oil."

Bruno pulls out a pencil and a piece of paper and scribbles Kiara's order down quickly and clumsily, nodding at Donnie after finishing.

"Make that two."

Bruno scribbles Donnie's order down in the same fashion and walks right into the back to prepare the sandwiches.

"It'll be a few minutes!"

Donnie nods as Bruno walks through a swinging door that leads into the back of the market. A few minutes later, Bruno emerges with two sandwiches wrapped in paper with two Frank's Black Cherry sodas. Donnie takes the two sandwiches and the sodas, handing them to Kiara.

"Hey, could you take these to the car for me? I wanna talk to Bruno real quick."

"Sure, Donnie. It was nice to meet you, Bruno."

"It was good meeting you too, sweetheart."

Kiara blushes even more as she walks back to the car.

"How much, Bruno?"

"Six bucks. Sodas on the house."

Donnie pulls out a ten and slips it into Bruno's pocket.

"Hey Donnie, gotta question for you."

"Yeah, what's up?"

"When are you guys planning on getting cigarettes again? I'm running low here, and people always come to me for cigarettes. You know when the next shipment will be?"

"Bruno...have we ever done you wrong? Are you not our first stop for this type of shit?"

Donnie can tell once he finishes talking to Bruno, Bruno feels embarrassed for asking him and Donnie feels bad for answering him in such a snarky tone.

"You're right. You're right. Sorry I asked, Donnie. I should've known. Tell your Pops I said hi."

"I will. Have a nice night, Bruno."

Donnie pulls another ten out of his hand and slips it into Bruno's pocket, as a small smile sprouts across his face. Donnie walks over to the car, hops in, and starts making way toward the Delaware River. Once bordering the river, they park on the edge of the river and hop out of the car and sit on the trunk, indulging themselves on the deliciousness of Bruno's sandwiches, all while watching the calmness of the river flow right under the magnificent night sky.

After finishing their sandwiches, they toss their trash away and head back to Kiara's place. After getting back to her place, they head up to her room and have a few drinks while watching TV in her living room when, all of a sudden, Donnie shoots up from the couch, wearing a look of concern that Kiara recognizes immediately.

"What's wrong?"

"Nothing, nothing. Just gotta make a call to work to let them know I won't be in. Forgot to let them know. You got a payphone around here?"

"Yeah, there's one half a block up my street."

"Thanks. I'll be right back."

Donnie hops up off the couch and practically sprints out of the door, walking all the way down to the ground floor and out the building. He looks at his watch, the clock reading 8:45 p.m. He looks up and down the street and, after spotting the payphone, makes his way toward it. He hops in the booth and scrounges for change in his pockets.

After looking through all of his pockets, he is finally able to find twenty cents needed for the call. He puts the coins in the slot, hearing the chinking and ringing of metal inside the machine, dialing up a number after he was finished. He puts the receiver to his ear and waits a few moments before a gruff voice answers the phone. "Eh?"

"Get me Pops."

"Eh."

A few silent seconds pass as Donnie looks at his watch before the phone is picked up again, this time by a more recognizable voice.

"What's up?"

"Sorry for the late call, but it just hit me while I was out. What are we gonna do about the rat?"

"Everything is taken care of. Don't worry about it. I'll fill you in soon."

With that, the call ends, and the dial tone hits Donnie's ear. He hangs up the payphone and walks back to Kiara's apartment. The whole call lasts about twenty seconds. Never go over thirty. That's the rule. It doesn't matter if it's your wife, your kid, your mother, or your goomah; nothing goes over thirty seconds on the phone. If it's that important, talk to them in person. Never ever the phone. That's how the cops get you.

After walking back to her apartment, he walks over to the couch and lays down on it, with Kiara laying down on him. After looking at him a few seconds, staring into his eyes, Donnie stares back with a childish smile to the likes of a schoolboy seeing his crush in the hallway.

"You're gorgeous."

Kiara bursts into a smile, and the two kiss passionately for a few minutes, pulling away only to take a breath. After that, Kiara lays her head on Donnie's chest, feeling his heartbeat on her ear as Donnie stares at the television blankly.

After a few minutes of silence, Donnie turns the TV off and wraps his arms around Kiara, pulling her close to his body. At that moment, Kiara feels safer than the gold in Fort Knox. She wraps her arms around his shoulders and neck, the couple slowly dozing off on her couch.

Right before she falls asleep, Donnie leans his head up and gently kisses her forehead, falling asleep quickly after it. After that kiss, Kiara knows he's the one. Kiara has fallen in love in his strong arms, close to his body, feeling his lips touch her face in a romantic sense of intimacy, wrapped up like sea otters on Kiara's living room couch.

XVII

All for Naught

They get married three weeks later, on September 8th, 1972, in Our Lady of Ransom church. Enzo and Stella are there, along with Maxo, Tino, Vinny Ruge, Badger, Sals, Sally Two, and all of the regulars from Mikey's. They honeymoon in Vegas, where Donnie meets a man by the name of Little Sammy.

Samuele D'Angelo Jr. was better known as Little Sammy. Little Sammy is a degenerate gambler and was a bastard of a human being as a young kid. His father, Sam Sr., is the president of the ILA before it was ripped away and handed to Franky Sigmund.

The cop have always been in Sam Sr.'s business ever since he became president. Nobody knows why; they just are. There are rumors of him being involved in the mafia or even being a head of a family in North Jersey, where his sizable Newark home is placed which is what originally tipped the cops off.

A few months after becoming president, Sam Sr. receives a large sum of unmarked bills totaling two million dollars as well as a million-dollar mansion in the suburbs of North Jersey after a bank heist in New York City. The cash, which is eventually found out about, is a cut of a sixteen-million-dollar cash heist from the Gamberini family out of New York. New York's don, Alfonso Gamberini, gets wind of the bank being available for a heist from one of the guards. This guard is being paid handsomely by Alfonso, and his job is to inform

Alfonso on when the bank will be most likely to have a successful heist. After about three months, the waiting has come to a close.

On July 6, 1958, at eight thirty in the morning three people— the Monticelli brothers, Dicky and Chrissy and Alfonso's son, Fonzie Gamberini—walk into Bank NYC and wait for the armor truck to arrive. All three men sit in the foyer and watch in silent pleasure as the armored truck rolls up in front of the bank and starts unloading bags of money.

After they unload about fifteen bags, all full of money, Dicky and Chrissy Monticelli put down their newspapers, get up, and walk out of the bank, with Fonzie in tow about fifteen feet behind them. As soon as they walk out, both brothers pull out their pieces and smack two of the guards on the back of their heads, knocking them unconscious.

A third guard walks out of the back of the truck and, seeing this, pulls his pistol and aims it right at Dicky's thick Sicilian mustache. Luckily, Fonzie sees this and fires a single shot from inside the bank. The shot is clean, quick, and precise. It shatters the bank window into a million pieces and scares the living shit out of all the bystanders and the tellers, but it whacks the third guard square between the eyes, who flops out of the truck, his head cracking open on the concrete road where his corpse now lays.

After subduing and taking care of all three guards, a white unmarked van pulls up right next to the trio of wise guys, who, one by one, begin tossing the bags into the van. After shoving in all of the bags, the three men hop in, and the car drives away from Bank NYC with lightning-quick speed.

In and out, the whole job takes around ten minutes, with the car finally pulling away from the bank around 8:39 a.m. It just so happens that after the heist, the owner of Bank NYC is given a payment of two million dollars to keep his mouth shut and not press charges by an insurance company that represented Bank NYC. This particular insurance company is run by none other than Alfonso Gamberini, and the owner of Bank NYC is none other than Sam D'Angelo Sr.

Now, this payment is filed legally as an insurance claim for the lost money, but two mil that is given to Sam Sr. is a cut from the original sixteen mil. After receiving his "insurance claim" by the bank, all the cops have to do is wait.

They wait for around a year, trying to hit Sam Sr. and the D'Ambrosio family on a RICO case that had been building. Eventually, the lead investigator for the FBI, Special Agent Lester Gallo, brings down hell on the Jersey mafia, leading to thirty-seven arrests of the D'Ambrosio family, one of them being the "supposed" head of the family, Sammy D'Angelo Sr.

They charge the family with practically every illegal activity in the book: from robbery, murder and racketeering to loitering and jaywalking. All thirty-seven members plead the fifth, with most of the wise guys and associates walking clean. Some of the members are convicted for contempt of court, but those are few and far between. All of it leads down to Sammy Sr., who pleads the fifth to every charge against him.

It looks like a convictionless case for Special Agent Gallo until he discovers Sammy Sr. never paid taxes on his "insurance claim." The next day in court, the day the case is to be dismissed, Special Agent Gallo gives the evidence to the prosecution, who swiftly brings forward the evidence to the judge. There is nothing Sammy can do.

He is tried and convicted for three counts of tax evasion, as when they found his insurance claim wasn't filed, two more claims from the bank weren't filed as well. Though it isn't as wildly as successful as Special Agent Gallo had hoped for, they got the big man of the D'Ambrosio family. Out of thirty-seven arrests, four men were convicted, the largest hit to the D'Ambrosio family being the boss himself.

The three men convicted for contempt of court serve their six months at a local county jail, hitting the street to get back to their bullshit with ease, while Sammy Sr. is stuck at Northern Jersey State Correctional Facility for the next fifteen years of his life. Franky Sigmund is given the presidential job shortly thereafter, due to Sam Sr.'s criminal tendencies.

After his transfer from civilian life to prison inmate, the D'Ambrosio crime family quickly gets back on its feet and, to avoid any trouble, sends Sammy Sr.'s son to Vegas to run their casino.

Before he gets on the jet en route to McKarmen Municipal Airport, Sammy is given several large duffel bags, being told to "have some fun" before leaving Jersey for good.

In those duffel bags is the remaining money from the Bank NYC Heist. All of the money ends up being invested in the well-being of the casino.

When Fonzie discovered this, Fonzie didn't like it at all. From the start, he wanted the sixteen mil all to himself. A week or so after the heist, Fonzie goes to his father and says Dicky is thinking about folding and ratting to the cops about the heist. Now, Dicky is a made guy, so normally, whacking him wouldn't be so simple. But when your father is the king of New York, you can get whatever the fuck you want. Less than twenty-four hours later, Dicky is gone. He is found two days later with a bullet in his right temple on the corner of Fifth and East Sixty-Ninth Street.

The cops rule it a suicide. Dicky is a lefty.

After his brother's death, Chrissy starts going off the rails crazy, thinking that if they whacked his brother, they can whack him too. To calm himself down, Chrissy goes to talk to Fonzie at a bar on East Twentieth Street. From the moment Chrissy walks into the bar to talk to Fonzie, he looks nuts. He keeps looking around the room like the NSA is wrapped around his neck and Fonzie isn't having it.

"Chrissy, what the fuck are you doing? Why are you looking everywhere like that? You tryin' to get yourself killed?"

"Sorry, Fonzie. I can't stop it. Ever since they whacked Dicky, I've been paranoid that I'm next."

"Wait, hold on, who's they?"

"What do you mean they? The fuckin' D'Ambrosio family—that's fuckin' they!"

"Hold the fuckin' phone, Chrissy. Why would the D'Ambrosios whack Dicky?"

"I don't fuckin' know, Fonzie. All I know is Dicky's gone, and I could be next." Just then, a light bulb goes off in Chrissy's head and a look of fear washes over his face. "Maybe...maybe this has something to do with the heist, Fonzie. Maybe the D'Ambrosios want the dough all to themselves, so they're whacking us one by one."

A light bulb goes off in Fonzie's head too, but instead of fear, a sinister look falls on Fonzie's face and a wicked smile forms in his mind.

"Oh shit. You may be right, Chrissy. They might be coming after us. We gotta get the fuck outta here and get on the lam."

Fonzie looks conspicuously around the bar and taps Chrissy lightly on the shoulder.

"Follow me. We'll head out the back, get to the car, and hit the mattresses."

Chrissy wholeheartedly agrees and follows Fonzie toward the back of the bar to a door that leads into an alleyway leading to East Twentieth. Fonzie walks up to the door and looks around the room quickly before opening the door that Chrissy walks through that leads to the alley. Fonzie walks out the door after Chrissy, and pretty much right as the door shuts, Chrissy is gone.

After getting about twenty feet down the alley, Fonzie walks up behind him, pulls out his piece, and cracks him twice in the nape of his skull, the blood splattering backward onto Fonzie's face like a Pollock painting. Chrissy's body drops fast, like turning off a light switch, his face crash landing on a mound of garbage-filled bags that rest in the alleyway, blood flowing down his neck and back, bleeding onto his jacket collar.

Fonzie is able to get out of the alley, but once he makes it onto the main road, he runs into a beat cop, who takes one look at him and tackles him to the ground. He gets pinched for Chrissy's murder and confessed to Dicky's murder, as well as confessing to the Bank NYC heist. While Fonzie confessed to the heist, he says he doesn't know where the money is, and even if he did, he isn't telling anyone.

Fonzie hoped that his father would use some of the sixteen mil to bail him out of jail, but Alfonso had given the D'Ambrosio family the lead to deal with the money. As a gift, the Gamberini family is given a measly 40 percent cut of the sixteen mil. The rest goes to the D'Ambrosio family.

After Alfonso hears what had happened to Dicky and Chrissy, he realizes what his son had become and walks away, leaving his only son to serve his forty-to-life prison sentence at Clint Correctional

Jail. Fonzie is barely twenty-one years old. He would have to wait until he is forty-six to be eligible for parole. Fonzie doesn't even last one week in the joint.

After five days, he manages to steal a belt from a prison guard office and hangs himself on a doorknob in the prison fitness room. Regardless, Fonzie would've been whacked anyways. After that, the remaining money mysteriously disappears, never to be seen or heard about again after its heist on the sweltering summer day in '58.

After getting the job and disappearing to Vegas, Sammy wizens up quickly. He cuts back on his alcohol consumption and completely stops gambling, going cold turkey from the second he steps foot in Nevada. Eventually, he turns to cigarettes to keep his gambling and alcohol addictions in check. After a few years, he is able to get a license and is now legally the head of the Adagirs Casino.

XVIII

Any Time after Midnight

Donnie and Kiara spend three weeks at the Adagirs. As a wedding gift, Enzo pays for everything. He gives Donnie and Kiara two hundred thousand cash before they leave for the airport, and they spend it all two weeks in. Donnie calls Enzo on a payphone about the cash situation or the lack thereof.

After getting off the phone, Enzo immediately calls up a business partner, who happens to be Sammy Jr. himself. As a wedding present, he sends the newlyweds a briefcase with one hundred thousand for their final week there. They spend about half by the week's end and decide to stay another week before heading back to Philly.

He is sitting at the craps table next to Kiara, who has five grand in the 30 to 1, with about another hundred grand on the side, waiting to bet. After going about thirty grand deep, she gets up and goes to the bathroom, and that's when Donnie sees her.

Her hair is a vibrant blond, but it compliments her miraculous blue eyes and her pristine white smile. Her figure conforms to the skintight gold dress that flows down to her knees, with an open strip running up the length of her thighs. Donnie spots her from across the room, and she spots him, the couple locking eyes and holding them still in a wave of infatuated passion. She smiles. Donnie smiles. She walks over to him and leans on his chair as Donnie looks over his shoulder to see if Kiara is coming back from the bathroom.

"Hey, handsome."

"Hi, how ya doin'?"

Donnie tries to look away, but he can't take his eyes off her. "What are you doing here?"

"I'm here on vacation. Taking a couple weeks here with my... girlfriend."

"Oh. Okay. You like Vegas?"

"Well, it certainly just got a lot better."

They both start laughing, and she leans in a little closer, placing the palm of her hand on the top of Donnie's left shoulder, beginning to caress it slightly. Suddenly, Donnie feels the slight touch of her lips as she leans in and whispers into his ear, "I could make your stay even better."

Donnie, who is looking at the table at the time, looks around slowly, making sure that Kiara isn't anywhere near the table.

"Where at?"

Slowly yet seductively, she reaches into a small pocketbook that she is holding in her other hand and pulls out a business card.

"You got a pen?"

Donnie reaches into his jacket pocket and pulls a pen, handing it to Sarah. Quickly but neatly, she writes down her hotel room number, slipping the business card into Donnie's hand before standing up straight.

"Any time after midnight. I'll be waiting—Sarah Sabine"

After that, she walks away from the craps table, leaving Donnie with a business card and a pleasant smile. A few seconds later, Donnie spots Kiara coming from the bathroom out of the corner of his eye and quickly pockets the card just as she sits down next to him.

"Did'ya win anything?"

"Nope. I didn't play. I was waiting for you to come back."

Kiara looks upset that Donnie didn't play a few times in her absence but quickly dismisses it as she moves the chips toward the betting area.

"Listen, I got a meeting tonight to talk about the stock market here in Vegas. I gotta take care of some stuff. We should probably get back to the room by quarter to midnight just to make sure I get there on time."

"But Donnie…it's already eleven thirty!"

"Hey, I gotta get to this meeting! It's important. We'll play a few more rounds, but after that, we gotta head back."

Kiara ughs loudly; and after a few more rounds, which end with her going down about fifty grand, Kiara and Donnie go up to their room, checking in at around eleven forty. Other than just fifty grand down, Kiara is also a few drinks down as well, the smell of rosé emanating from her breath and body as Donnie lays her in their penthouse room suite bed. As he lays her down, just before he left, Kiara wraps her tired drunken arms around Donnie's neck and whispers, "I love you, Donnie."

Donnie looks at Kiara, his newly wedded wife, and kisses her, tasting the alcohol and sweet love in her lips. After that, he tucks her tired body under the covers and leaves the hotel room. Just as he leaves, he pulls the business card and flips it over, seeing Room 215 scribbled neatly on the back of the card.

After reading the room number, he tucks it back into his pocket and walks down the hallway to a stairwell, walking down to the lobby where Little Sammy and the Vegas guys are shooting the shit and making small talk, all while smoking cigarettes and talking about their first years working as an wise guy back home East. Donnie, visibly flustered, comes walking up to Sammy.

"Whoa, Donnie. You doing okay? Did'ya wife suck your dick the wrong way?"

The whole table starts roaring with laughter, which helps calm Donnie down a little bit as he chuckles at the remark. "Yeah, I'm good, Sammy. I just gotta talk to you about something."

Sammy, smirking heavily, places a cigarette in his mouth and nods at the guys with a be-right-back look and walks about fifteen yards away from the table.

"What's up, Donnie?"

"I need you to clip someone."

Sammy is mid-drag when Donnie starts his claim, and it doesn't even faze him. He finishes his cigarette pull and blows the smoke away before speaking.

"Okay. Who do you wanna clip?"

"A chick."

"Oh. Not likely, Donnie. Unless she tried to fuck you, I can't do anything."

"Well, that's exactly what she did. I just laid my new wife to bed. I'm walking down the hallway to go back down to the casino to have a little fun, and this dumb blonde broad comes practically out of left field as I'm walking starts talking to me. We talk for a few seconds; get each other's name; and then out of nowhere, she grabs me, forces me up against the wall, starts groping me and unbuckling my belt. I'm sitting here trying to have a good honeymoon with my new wife. We've been married for two weeks, and this whore tries to fuck me in the hallway of your casino. I'm not having my marriage ruined by some fuckin' bitch!"

Sammy is sitting there, peacefully listening to Donnie go on about his particular dilemma. After he finishes, Sammy takes a drag of his cigarette and places the butt in an ashtray adjacent to his hand.

"All right. Did you get her name? You said you got her name."

"Yeah, it was Sarah something. Sabine, I think. Yeah, Sarah Sabine."

In that moment, Sammy's eyes roll so far back into his head, his veins show more than the white of his eyes.

"Aw shit. Not fuckin' her again."

"What does that mean?"

"Sarah Sabine is a broad that's been here for about a decade or so. Her boss is Ricky Calderone, who was a captain to Vegas Don Antonio 'Tony M' Madaro. Now, we have no problem with Tony M since he's a don in name only, but he's technically under payroll of Alfonso Gamberini. Ricky C doesn't give two shits. Ricky C is in charge of the prostitutes here in Vegas. We gave him absolute freedom to tell his girls to do what they wanted or what they needed to do.

"Our only rule to him, especially in my casino, was to stay away from the newlyweds and, most importantly, the newly wedded wise guys because if you fuck with the wrong wise guy, you get whacked. End of story. Eventually, I kicked him out of my casino. But one of his girls, this Sarah bitch, keeps coming back. We kick her out, but some fuckin' how, she just keeps coming back. I think it's time we kick her out for good."

And just like that, Sammy turns around, facing the table full of his guys. He whistles twice in a loud, successive manner, and like dogs, they rise from the table and follow Sammy. Sammy leads his wise guys and Donnie through the casino floor, leading them to the counting room where they count all the money that comes their way. In the counting room is a door that leads to the meeting room, where Sammy and his wise guys meet every night to discuss the casino and go over any issues. Normally, they'd be issues that reside between a customer getting a bad drink or a problem with room service.

Tonight is different.

Tonight, Little Sammy, his wise guys, and Donnie will be taking care of Sarah Sabine for good. Donnie looks down at his watch, reading 12:03 a.m. All he thinks about is Sarah's scribbled writing on the business card.

"Any time after midnight."

XIX

Room 215

Donnie, Sammy, and his wise guys all walk into the meeting room with blank faces, either smoking cigarettes or sipping on whiskey glasses. The room is minimal, with a singular, circular table with a few ashtrays scattered on it sitting in the middle of the room. In the back corner from the entrance to the room lies a tattered sack. After the eight or so men enter the room, they all sit down accordingly, with Donnie sitting adjacent to Sammy Jr., his wise guys sitting down around the table.

"All right, everyone. Donnie has come to me tonight, asking that I ice someone for him. It turns out our girl Sarah Sabine is back again. Sarah tried to fuck Donnie here in my casino hallways. I want her gone for good this time. Do we have any information of where she might be?"

After a few silent seconds, Donnie fumbles through the content of his pockets and pulls out the business card that holds Sarah Sabine's scribbled writing.

"Well...after she tried to fuck me and I pushed her off, she seemed to have been turned on by it and told me to come to Room 215 any time after midnight."

Sammy nods slowly as he pulls out a cigarette and lights a match, taking a few puffs before answering Donnie.

"And what time is it now?"

All the wise guys simultaneously turn their wrists, flashing their golden and diamond-studded watches as they check the time.

"All right. It's about a quarter after twelve. Let's get ready. I want this done and over with before one. Get the bag."

After finishing, one of the wise guys stands up and walks over to the back corner. This particular wise guy was a built Sicilian hitman by the name of Paulie Clericuzo.

Paulie is an expert. He has been Sammy's go-to man whenever trouble needs to be taken care of. Paulie was Sammy's bodyguard when he moved to Vegas in '59, and over the past thirteen years, Paulie is responsible for one hundred missing people in Clark County, as well as one hundred graves dug in the Mojave Desert. At night, the desert is as black as it is barren. If you fuck up in Vegas, you stay in Vegas, resting eternally under six feet of Nevada sand. There are many holes in that desert, each with a certain reason to have been dug. Tonight, one more hole will be placed in the everlasting Nevadan graveyard.

Paulie slaps the bag on the table as Sammy pulls the drawstrings to open the sack.

An entire arsenal of weapons explodes onto the table: .22s, .25s, .38s, machine pistols, hand grenades, as well as a variety of knives and brass knuckles. Paulie reaches into the bag, grabbing a .38, sticking it into the waistband of his undergarments, and a .45, sticking it into the small of his back.

Paulie pushes the bag in the direction of Donnie, who looks back and forth between Paulie and the bag.

"Go on. Pick a card, any card!"

Paulie's quick remark leads to a few brash chuckles around the table. Donnie nods his head as a smile stretches across his rosy Irish cheeks. After staring at the bag for a few seconds, he grabs the bag and pulls it over to him. He reaches into the bag blindly, touching the inside of the bag, feeling the metallic clinks of the guns. After feeling around for the minute, Donnie pulls out an Uzi, chambered-in 9mm. He then reaches to the small of his back, pulling out his revolver.

"Ooh, a king and a queen!"

Paulie chuckles, still going off the card theme for the pieces. After Donnie pulls his guns out, Sammy closes the bag and places it back into the corner.

"All right. Here's how it'll go down. Paulie, Donnie, head up to her room in ten minutes. Two of my other guys will drive out there and start digging. It shouldn't take longer than a half hour for these two guys to dig a nice ditch for our girlfriend upstairs. After getting to her room, incapacitate her. Do not kill her. I don't want no blood or bodies in my casino. Saving the killing for the desert. After getting her unconscious, take the emergency stairwell down to the basement garage. Someone will be waiting there with the car."

Sammy takes one more look at his watch, the clock reading 12:20 a.m.

Forty minutes left.

"All right. Go take care of business."

Paulie nodded and got up off the table, Donnie in tow quickly behind him.

As Paulie and Donnie enter the counting room, Donnie hears the creaks of the chairs as the two wise guys bound for the dessert stand up to leave the room.

After making it to the casino floor, Paulie and Donnie head to the elevator as the two wise guys head out the door of the casino. Paulie taps the up arrow on the pad adjacent to the doors and the pair step back, watching the arrow move slowly from floor fifteen all the way down to the ground floor. After pausing momentarily, the doors open, revealing an empty elevator cabin.

Paulie and Donnie walk onto the platform, and Paulie grunts at Donnie, motioning him to push the button. Donnie does so, and moments later, they feel the elevator shift in movement and rise two floors up, dumping the wise guys on the second floor. They hop off the elevator and walk down the hall, turning the corner as they spot Room 215 a few more doors down. Donnie feels the sweat running down his forehead and neck, dripping down to the small of his back, combining with the metal of the Uzi stuck down his back waistband.

After walking a few more doors, Paulie and Donnie are standing in front of Room 215, staring at the door with a silent, deadly look.

After a few seconds, Paulie knocks on the door twice, the loud bangs echoing down the empty hallway.

Quickly, Paulie covers up the peephole with his large meat slab of a hand as he hears footsteps walk over to the entrance of the door.

"Who is it?"

To Donnie's surprise, the voice is a man's. The shock covers his face momentarily before he shakes it off.

"Room service for Room 215."

After a few quick moments of silence, the door's deadbolt unlocks, and a man starts to speak as he opens the door, peeking his head through the cracked slit.

"Listen, buddy, I think you got the wrong fuckin' ro—"

In a sudden burst of energy, Paulie kicks the door in, the door connecting with the man's nose, breaking it entirely. The man falls back limp, belly up on the bedroom carpet floor, blood slowly beginning to run out of his nostrils and down his cheeks, pooling next to his earlobes. Paulie and Donnie bust into the door, pulling out their pieces in case any other danger is imminent. After seeing the mystery man on the floor, they lower their weapons and sigh in disgust.

"Ah shit. What the fuck did Sammy say? No blood on the fuckin' floor!"

"I didn't mean to crack his nose. I meant to fuckin' bump him away from the door."

"Bump him away? You ran into the door like a fuckin' bull!"

After arguing for a few seconds, Donnie notices a scampering sound by the bed, about ten feet in front of them. Donnie gets Paulie's attention, but before they can even react, a fairly dressed woman clutching a .44 comes out into the open and fires a quick shot, one that barely misses Paulie's thick neck. Before the woman can get off a second shot, Donnie fires his gun once, striking the woman square between the eyes. Her body becomes stunned for a moment before collapsing lifelessly to the floor. After firing the shot, Paulie immediately goes into a fit of quiet rage.

"Shit! Fuck! Aw fuck. Sammy's gonna kill us. Fuck!"

Paulie places his hand on his head, trying to figure out what to do. Donnie walks over to the woman and looks at her face, still as beautiful as when he saw it a few hours earlier, with the exception of the bullet hole that lay between her perfectly detailed eyebrows. While Donnie walks toward Sarah's corpse, Paulie kneels over and places his fingers over the man's neck, checking for a pulse. After feeling for a few seconds, he stands up even angrier than when he kneeled down.

"Perfect...he's fuckin' dead too!"

Even though Donnie knows Paulie is sweating out his ass and livid as anything, Paulie keeps his composure well, pacing the room to try forming the beginnings of a plan in our head. After a few seconds of quick pacing around the room, staring back and forth between Sarah and the man, his face lights up with an idea.

"Grab the fuckin' curtains, lay them on the floor, lay the bed-sheets on top of them, and then we'll place the bodies on top of them. The different layers will help hold the blood and not soak the car trunk."

Donnie nods and walks over to the balcony, ripping the presumably expensive curtains off the rail. He rolls them up in his arms and then lays them semi straight on the bedroom floor. After straightening them, Donnie walks over to the beds, removing their sheets and laying them on top of the curtains as Paulie places his piece in the small of his back and begins to move the man. As he lifts his arms, Donnie walks over and grabs his legs, the two men placing his body on the sheets, Sarah's body following suit. After dropping her body on top of his, Donnie's face becomes washed with uncertainty.

"Fuck, Paulie, how are we gonna get them down to the basement without people noticing?"

"Same way Sammy said if we didn't kill them. Emergency stairwell. That'll lead right to the basement. We got a car waiting there for us. Come on. Let's get the fuck outta here before actual room service comes."

Donnie nods and grabs one end of the sheet collection, Paulie grabbing the other. After both men form firm grips on the curtain, they simultaneously lift up and make their way out of Room 215, turning left down the hallway toward the emergency exit stairwell. For the most part, nobody ever uses this stairwell except for maybe a few maintenance people who don't feel like waiting for the elevator on busy nights.

After making it inside the emergency stairwell entrance, they begin their descent to the basement. It's only three floors to the basement garage, but when you're carrying about three hundred pounds of dead weight, it's not an easy trip. Luckily, they make it down to the basement a few minutes later, Donnie poking his head out to make sure the car is there, as well as checking for any witnesses that can see what they're doing. After looking around the garage suspiciously for a few glances, they exit the stairwell. A car slowly pulls up to Donnie and Paulie, driven by another one of Sammy's wise guys.

"Pop the trunk!"

After a few seconds, he hops out of the driver's seat, walks around to the back, and unlocks the trunk, popping the lip up, revealing a spacious barren area for the bodies. Donnie and Paulie walk over to the trunk and lay the two bodies down, covering them with the remaining cloth.

"Oh shit. Are they dead, Paulie?"

"No…they were a little tired while we were walking them down, so we ripped the curtains off their room and carried them down so they could rest a little longer. Yes, they're dead, you fuckin' asinine prick!"

The wise guy, who can't be older than twenty-two, gulps loudly and walks away quickly from Paulie, hopping in the driver's seat. Donnie shuts the trunk and hops in the passenger seat with Paulie hopping in the back. As the car starts up and he makes his way out of the garage, the young wise guy looks at Paulie and say quietly, "Sammy ain't gonna be happy about this, Paulie."

"Oh, shut the fuck up! They were gonna die anyways. Fuck's the difference?"

To that, he shrugs and makes his way out of the strip, the car disappearing into the infinite darkness of the desert night. After driving for about three minutes, the driver notices a quick flash of light, resembling car headlights about a quarter mile away on his left. He looks at it again; and they flash again, once, twice, three times.

After the third time, the driver makes way toward the flash. As he gets closer, he meets with a car, with two of Sammy's wise guys standing next to it, holding shovels, with a hole about three feet away from the car. As Paulie spots the hole, he rolls down the window and begins talking to one of the diggers.

"Make it bigger."

After Paulie says this, one of the men smirks and chuckles as he places a cigarette into his mouth.

"Jesus, Donnie. Did'ya almost get fucked by a whale?"

The two diggers start laughing, but Paulie's face remains emotionless. "Make it fuckin' bigger."

Paulie takes a quick glance at his watch, his face becoming slightly red.

"It's a quarter of one. Let's get this fuckin' hole done and get the fuck outta here."

The men sigh but listen to Paulie, walking over to the hole and continuing to dig. After about a few minutes of digging, Paulie hops out of the car and taps on Donnie's door, signaling him to get out as well. Donnie does so; and the pair walk to the trunk, unlock it, and grab the curtain-concealed bodies. They carry them over to the hole and drop them in it, their bodies crumpled together in their Nevadan grave. After staring at the bodies for a few seconds, Donnie reaches around the small of his back and pulls out his Uzi, cranking the charging handle back, loading a round.

"Just makin' sure."

Paulie nods slowly as Donnie opens fire on the desert grave, round after round flying into the two bodies, sinking into their arms, legs, stomachs, faces, chests—blood flowing like a leaky faucet from their many wounds. After emptying the magazine, Donnie looks at the gun and tosses it on top of the bodies, walking back toward the car.

Paulie stares at Donnie for a moment before looking at the diggers, nodding once as they begin to fill the whole again. It only takes a few minutes before the four wise guys are on their way back to the Adagirs Casino, their watches hitting one as they pull up to the front of the casino. Sammy is waiting out front, waiting for them to pull up, and once they exit the car and spot Sammy looking at them, Paulie nods once. Sammy nods back and walks back into the casino. Donnie heads up to his room and sleeps like a baby. He always sleeps well after clipping someone. Donnie and Kiara go home to Philly a few days later.

Kiara never knew about the job or Sarah Sabine. If she did, she didn't care. Donnie cared. Donnie's heart, for the first time in his life, wasn't 100 percent about going through with a hit. He doesn't know why it isn't, but it isn't. After the hit, Donnie feels like he is slipping, not quickly, but slowly slipping. The scary thing is that he doesn't see where he's slipping toward.

After getting home, Donnie doesn't do anything. He doesn't get out of bed, doesn't go to work, nothing. He lays in his room, motionlessly sick and tired. After about a week, he gets up and leaves the house, heading to Mikey's to see the guys for the first time in over a month since he got married. After talking to the guys for a few minutes, catching up about events in Philly, he walks downstairs to the basement right into his Pop's office. Right as he walks in, he knows something is off. Enzo isn't upset or mad, but he isn't showing any emotion, which is much worse than showing something.

"Hey, Donnie. Good to see you here again."

Maxo Salucci, one of Enzo's captains, is sitting in the room too, smoking a cigar.

"Hey, Maxo."

"How's it going, Donnie?"

"Please have a seat."

Donnie feels like a child in trouble. He isn't scared of what could happen, but he is curious of what Enzo wants of him. "What's up, Pops?"

After taking a second to clear his throat, Enzo looks at his adopted son with a look of seriousness and with a twinkle of fear in his eye.

"We've been waiting for you to get back to do this. I'm glad you had fun on your honeymoon, and I hope you and Kay do fantastic as a couple. Maybe even bring me a few grandchildren. But right now, it's time to get back to work. We need you to take point on taking care of Figs. Even though you're not made, Sammy Jr. informed me of what you did on your honeymoon, and I'm proud of you, Donnie. Me and Maxo will give you the details tonight on what's to go down. Go upstairs and catch up with the guys."

Enzo and Maxo stand up, Enzo shaking his son's hand quickly before bringing him in for a brief hug. After pulling away, Maxo and Donnie shake hands, and Donnie leaves Enzo's basement office, going upstairs to talk to the guys about his adventures in Vegas.

XX

Nothing Too Complicated

After spending the remainder of the day with the guys, Donnie heads back to Enzo's basement office to talk about what they're going to do with Figs. Maxo and Enzo are sitting there, conversing amongst themselves quietly as Donnie walks calmly into the room.

"Ah, Donnie. Sit down. Let's get down to business."

Donnie sits down as Enzo stands up to pace around the room as he often does when he explains his jobs.

"Now, you know about our warehouse that we normally run our business through, correct?"

"Yeah Pops, the one off of Schuylkill Avenue, right?"

Maxo Salucci, silently smoking a cigar, interjects on the conversation. "That's the one."

"We got a shipment of cigarettes coming into that warehouse along with a line of suits and dress, all designer, as well as a jewelry shipment later that evening, around nine. You, Maxo, Sally Two, Vinny Ruge, Figs, and Sals will head to the warehouse at midnight, just when everything has died down and the workers get lazy.

"Youse guys are gonna rob the joint. Even though we run the warehouse, we're gonna make it look like a robbery. I have a Teamster driver set to arrive at the location at five after. I want you busting into that place at midnight on the fuckin' tick. While you, Maxo, and Sally Two unload the swag and cigs into the truck, Sals will take Figs to the river's edge to have a 'fatherly talk' with him. After talking to him for a few minutes…"

Enzo holds his hand with his index finger and thumb extended in imitation of a gun.

"Sals will clip Figs. I talked to him personally about it, and if he was 100 percent about doing this since Figs was practically his son. He said that if anyone was going to whack Figs, it might as well be him. I've directed him to fire three shots and three shots only. One in each lung and one in the head. If you hear more than three shots, grab as much swag as you can and get the fuck outta there. Reminder that it's still a normal job. We just gotta take care of some other business as well. The whole job should be less than an hour to an hour. Remember, when you're dropping off the cigarette shipments, you know who comes first, capisce?"

Donnie nods as he pulls out a cigarette and lights it, taking a few drags and blowing the smoke in the direction of the door.

"When is this all going down?"

"Tonight. The cigarettes and the suits are already there."

Enzo turns his wrist to look at his watch, the time reading 7:35 p.m.

"Dresses should be there too, and the jewelry is coming in a little over an hour. Get the guys and get ready. Remember your fuckin' masks and remember to make it look like a robbery. Get the fuck outta here."

Maxo nods and stands up, with Donnie following him out of the office and upstairs to the barroom where Vinny Ruge, Sally Two, Sals, and Figs are. Donnie waits at the top of the steps as Maxo walks over to the group of men, and after a few moments, they all turn on their heels and make their way toward the basement.

Donnie walks into the basement meeting room where the guys play cards after the busy night. As Donnie enters the room, he stares at the floor, where a faint bloodstain still remains from when he drunkenly clipped Joey Slur, the same night Books got whacked by the Mazzante family. Four guys all sit down at a circular table while Maxo walks over to a large briefcase that's sitting in the corner.

He grabs it, walks back over to the table, and places it down. He pops the case and flips it over as a waterfall of firearms flows is dumped from the case. Ferocious smiles instantly sprout around the table as they all start grabbing and looking at the weapons. As they are occupied, Maxo walks back over to the corner, dropping the briefcase and grabbing a large drawstring bag, walking over to the guys and dumping its contents on the table. This time, a slew of automatic rifles, pistols, and explosives falls from the bag, the table erupting with cheers and whistles.

"Just pick your pieces and let's go over the plan."

Maxo drops the bag and sits down next to Donnie as he grabs an automatic rifle and also checks to make sure his signature is still there on his back. The others grab .32s, .38s and Uzis, sticking them in their jacket pockets, pants pockets, ankle holsters, the smalls of their backs, or the crotches of their pants.

"All right. Let's go over the plan, just to make sure youse don't fuck it up. Enzo already told us that the truck is gonna get to the warehouse at midnight. I wanna be there at least five before, if not ten before midnight. There shouldn't be a lot of people there at that time, about maybe ten to fifteen guys, more than we have, but we're going in armed. If we catch them at the right moment, none of them won't have time to go to their offices and grab their guns because I know for certain that the boss of the warehouse has one.

"After we bust into the place, there's a break room on the first floor. Vinny and I will usher and keep the crew in there and make sure they don't do nothing they'll regret. Sals, you, Donnie, Sally Two, and Figs will start grabbing the swag and loading it into the truck when he gets there. After loading the swag, we'll lock the employees in the break room and get the fuck out of there. Nothing too complicated. We've all had jobs like these before. Tonight is no different."

Maxo looks down at his watch, the time reading 8:03 p.m.

"All right, gentlemen. Go upstairs and rest a bit. We got time. We'll be getting outta here by about twenty-five before twelve. Get a drink. Calm yourselves. I gotta talk to Enzo. Get the fuck outta here."

Almost as a group, the men stand up from their chairs and leave the room. All the pistols they chose are on their person, but the rifles and machine pistols are kept downstairs so as not to draw suspicion by the bar patrons. For the next few hours, they will all be sitting at the bar, watching TV, shooting the shit, drinking, or a little bit of all three. It was a cool Saturday night in October. College football is on, and everyone is invested in the game, especially those who have money on them. USC was playing Stanford that night, and that game had everyone on the edge of their seats.

Everyone except Donnie.

For Donnie, all he can think about Kiara and how they had gotten married almost exactly a month prior. Then, his mind jumps to the present moment, a routine job with a twist only Maxo, Sals, and Enzo know about. Donnie asks the bartender for a shot of whiskey, expressionlessly watching him place a shot glass on a coaster in front of him. Donnie watches as the whiskey flows slowly from the liquor pourer, the ceiling lights bouncing off it as the bartender pulls the bottle away from the glass.

Donnie nods at him; and in one crisp motion, he lifts the glass, dumps the bitter liquid into his mouth, and swallows it, placing the glass back on the counter with a light smack. After that, he watches the game with the guys, smoking the occasional cigarette and taking a shot here and there to pass the time. Eventually, time passes, and Maxo walks up the basement steps to the bar floor, looking at the guys all sitting at the bar, staring at the TV with wonder comparable to a child at his first ball game.

Donnie spots Maxo, and Maxo nods, exiting back down to the basement. Donnie taps on Vinny Ruge's shoulder and nods at him. Vinny drains his shot and takes one final drag of his cigarette before standing up and telling the rest of the guys. All of the guys drain their shots as if it would be their last and follow Vinny and Donnie downstairs to the basement. Maxo is standing at the bottom of the stairwell, smoking a cigarette and sipping on a glass of scotch. Just like the guys, he takes one more drag and finishes his glass.

Even on a routine job like this, you never know if you're coming back. You take every drag of a cigarette, every sip of alcohol, and every breath as if it will be your last.

After finishing his glass, Maxo leads the men into the meeting room and they all strap up, loading their firearms and checking their magazines. While the guys do that, Maxo grabs a box full of ski masks, handing them off one by one to the guys.

"Me and Sals will be driving. Vinny, you come with me. Sals, you take Donnie, Sally Two, and Figs. Routine job, gentlemen. Nothing too serious. If youse just take your time, we all should be in bed with our wifes tonight. Or our goomahs. Doesn't matter to me."

Maxo's sly remark draws some chuckles amongst the group. Maxo peers at his watch, the time reading 11:37 p.m.

"All right. Let's get the fuck outta here."

The guys all leave the bar through a basement exit that leads up to an alleyway adjacent to the street. Both cars are parked in the alley, Maxo's in the front and Sals behind his. The six men get into their respective cars and start them, the low rumble of the engines beating the walls of the alleyway. Seconds later, both cars are out of the alleyway, riding down the street, turning onto Girard shortly after. They cruise down Girard for about a mile and a half, turning onto Broad, the two-car caravan coasting under the clear night sky.

In Sals's car, Sals is driving. Figs is riding shotgun with Donnie and Sally Two riding the back. About a mile down Broad, stuck at a long red light, Sals starts fidgeting with his piece, looking at the trigger and the hammer and the cylinder. After a few seconds, Sals sighs and turns his head, halfway facing Donnie.

"Yo, Donnie. Could we swap pieces? Mine's acting all screwy, and I know you're good with guns. Maybe you could fix it or something."

Donnie, not wanting to disobey a made man's order, takes Sals's gun. Just as he grabs Sals's gun, the light goes green and Sals starts driving.

"Hand it to Figs 'cause I gotta drive. See if there's something wrong with it."

Donnie tosses Figs his piece and starts inspecting Sals's gun as they start driving around City Hall, William Penn looking down majestically over the City of Brotherly Love.

Donnie starts looking at the gun, not able to see much in the dark of night, only getting a glimpse every few seconds from the streetlights. By the time he gets a clear, definitive look at it, both cars have turned off South Street and are pulling into the warehouse parking lot off Schuylkill Avenue. Donnie sticks the piece into his underwear waistband and looks at his watch, the time reading 11:53 p.m.

Perfect timing.

Maxo and Vinny exit the car, one hand on their rifles and the other pulling down the ski mask, covering everything except their eyes and mouth. The pair racks their rifles, and Sals's car empties, the four guys racking their AKs and Uzis. Maxo and Vinny are about ten feet ahead of them as they walk in a quickened pace toward the warehouse door. Maxo kicks the door in with Vinny practically glued to his back as the four men hear muffled shouts from Maxo Salucci's thick Sicilian voice. "Get on the ground! Get on the fuckin' ground now! Get on the fuckin' ground!"

Just as the four men enter the warehouse, Vinny and Maxo are ushering the warehouse workers into the break room, one of them holding his face with blood pouring out of his nose. Donnie looks down and spots a .38 revolver lying on the ground twenty feet away.

"One of these fucks had a piece on him. Luckily, he wasn't a quick draw. He got a noseful of my fuckin' buttstock as a gift for that one. That's all of them. Me and Vinny will keep them here."

After the four enter and gaze around the warehouse, the loud squeal of truck breaks pierce through the air like a whistle.

"That's our guy. Pop the door and grab the shit."

Donnie and Sally Two walk over to the large warehouse doors, standing about fifteen feet high, and they swing them outward, the light from the inside of the warehouse cutting into the night as the truck backs up to the warehouse. Sally Two walks up to the truck door and flings it upward, revealing its barren insides.

Sally hops into the truck as Donnie, Sals, and Figs start grabbing dressing racks full of designer suits and dresses; containers full of expensive shoes and heels; racks and racks filled with diamond, sapphire, ruby, emerald, and gold jewelry, ranging from bracelets to earrings to rings; and of course, an entire shipping container's worth of MC Cigarettes, the best in the nation.

As Donnie is grabbing a master case of MCs, he watches as Sals has his hand draped over Figs, walking out of the warehouse. Donnie looks at Maxo, who looks at him and with a solemn stare. They each nod once.

Sals walks around the side of the warehouse, so the driver cannot see them, to the river's edge with Figs, the two men laughing and reminiscing about times past.

"Remember that one time when you took me to play ball at the fields and I accidentally tossed the ball into the bushes, and when you went to get it, you ended up getting poison ivy?"

The pair start laughing harder as Sals pulls out two cigars, handing one to Figs.

"Oh, you bet I remember. I'm still fuckin' itching my balls from that one."

Sal places the cigar into his mouth, lighting it up and taking a few puffs in the process. Figs sticks his cigar in his mouth, Sals moving the lighter from his cigar to Figs, who takes a few puffs as the flame hovers over his cigar.

"You remember that time where I had just come home from the bar. You had been living with us for a few years by then. You were sitting at home with Momma, eating cereal and watching the Tonight Show, laughing your ass off. You must've been around eighteen, nineteen years old by that point. I walked into the kitchen to grab some food and when I walked back in the living room, both of youse were laughing, and I just stood there and looked at you and started smiling. That right there was the happiest moment of my life, watching you and Ma laugh at the TV so purely and so joyfully. It made me realize how much I love youse both. How much I love you."

Just then, Sals starts sniffling, holding back tears; but the sniffles grow louder and louder. Figs notices this and turns his body, which was facing the river, toward Sals, his adoptive father.

"Ay, Pops, it's okay. I love you too."

Figs places a hand on Sals's shoulder, staring at him for a few moments before leaning in for a tight hug. Figs's embrace increases the intensity of the tears as Sals slides his hand behind his back, wrapping his hand around the grip of Donnie's revolver. Sals, still tightly embracing his son, whispers into Figs' ear those three devastating words.

"I'm sorry, Figlio."

XXI

Front Page in Bold

Maxo is looking around the room, his gun holstered in the crook of his elbow, the barrel scanning the room like a sentry gun. The warehouse workers are all on their knees, staring at Maxo and Vinny with looks of fear, anger, and sadness.

His view pans over to two workers sitting down next to the worker whose nose is bleeding even more profusely than it was before. One worker is rubbing a hand on his shoulder, the other holding a roll of paper towels, a small bloody pile of them accumulating next to the trio of workers. It's been about five minutes since Sals and Figs left the warehouse for the river's edge. He peers over his shoulder to see Donnie and Sally Two loading boxes into the truck trailer. Everything is going smoothly. Just as planned.

Suddenly, a gunshot pierces the air. Luckily, it is outside the warehouse.

Just as planned.

Sally Two, who is inside the trailer, pulls out his piece and ducks further into it. Donnie ducks and pulls out Sals' revolver. He motions for Sally to stay in the trailer while he goes and investigate. In quick succession, two more shots follow, each one equally as loud and brain shaking.

Just as planned.

Donnie walks over toward the door when a fourth shot rings out. Donnie's face drains of color as he looks at Maxo, whose face is also drained of color. Maxo taps Vinny with the muzzle of his gun and motions to leave. Vinny runs out of the room, and Maxo raises the buttstock to his cheek, walking backward toward the door.

Once he's through the doorway, he closes the door shut, locking it and in one quick motion, and slams the end of his buttstock into the doorknob, snapping it clean off. The driver has had his head down since the first shot rang out. Sally Two is in the back of the trailer as Vinny hops into the back, gun raised slightly in case the workers break free. Maxo hops into the trailer, Donnie following suit a few seconds later.

After all four men are in the trailer, they wait a few seconds for Sals to emerge from the side of the warehouse. Thirty seconds come and go. Sals is nowhere to be seen. Donnie looks over at Maxo, who sighs loudly. In a reluctant manner, Maxo taps the side of the truck twice and the truck slowly pulls away from the warehouse, disappearing in the crystal-clear night.

The truck maneuvers its way back to Fishtown, stopping only at Bruno's Italian Market for the night to drop off his cigarette shipments. The rest of the deliveries would be made tomorrow. Normally, the guys would make their shipments the night of a warehouse trip, but after tonight, Enzo would want to hear from them what happened and what went wrong.

When they get back to the bar, Maxo, Donnie, Sally, and Vinny all go down to Enzo's basement office with looks of fear and disappointment across their faces, like kids preparing to be scolded by their parents. Enzo is sitting in his large office chair, smoking a cigar when the four men enter the room.

Enzo raises his hand calmly, looking at Vinny and Sally, nodding his head once. Seeing this, Sally and Vinny nod back, leaving the room accordingly, leaving Donnie, Maxo and Enzo alone in the office. After Sally exits, Maxo walks over to the office door, shutting it closed and locking it tight. For a few seconds, everything is pitch quiet, the sound of the burning and crinkling of cigar paper becoming the sole sound emitted from the trio. After a few more slow puffs,

Enzo removes the cigar from his mouth and places it on an ashtray. "Where's Sals?"

Donnie looks at Maxo, who looks at him, each with a look of confusion. After a moment, they both shrug and Enzo snaps.

"What the fuck do you mean, you don't know where Sals is? Was he not fuckin' with you? I expected five men to walk through that door tonight, yet only four of you are here. Why is that, Maxo?"

Donnie, sweating harshly, interjects Enzo with a hurried manner in his voice. "Pops, we don't really know, we just—"

Enzo's hand shoots up, Donnie's voice cowering down to silence. "Maxo, what the fuck happened?"

"Everything was going perfectly. We got there when we needed to, busted into the place, took care of the warehouse workers—"

"Took care of them how?"

"Well, one of them had a piece on them but wasn't quick enough to pull it out. I cracked him across the nose with my stock, and he fell down. That seemed to straighten out the other workers. Me and Vinny ushered all of them into the break room while Donnie, Sally, Figs and Sals started moving the swag. The truck pulled in right on schedule, and the four of them started loading the swag onto the truck.

"After about maybe five minutes, Sals took Figs outside the warehouse to do his stuff. I guess they must've been talking or something 'cause it wasn't until five to ten minutes later that the first shot rang out. A few seconds passed, and two more rang out. Three shots. Just as you told Sals.

"Then about thirty seconds later, a fourth shot rang out. You told him three shots, so when I heard the fourth, we got the fuck outta there. The warehouse workers were all locked inside the break room when we pulled away. We even waited a few minutes to see if Sals was coming. After that, we just left and headed back here. That's all, Enzo."

Enzo is sitting in his chair, looking contemplatively at his captain as he explains what happened. After Maxo finishes, Enzo swings his gaze over at Donnie.

"Donnie, is that what happened?"

Without speaking, Donnie slowly nods his head.

Enzo drops his head, sighing heavily. "Neither of you have yet to answer me my initial question. Where...the fuck...is Sals?"

"He's either alive and hurt, went rogue, and is on the lam or dead."

"Well, fuckin' figure out which one is it!" Enzo's face is now beet red with anger. "Get the fuck outta my office!"

Emotionless, Donnie and Maxo leave Enzo's office and head to the meeting room, where Vinny and Sally are presumably playing cards to calm themselves down. Before entering the room, Donnie talks to Maxo about the Sals's incident.

"How the fuck are we gonna find out what happened to Sals?"

Maxo looks down at his watch, the time reading one thirty in the morning.

"The workers have a phone in the back corner of the break room. I saw it while you unloaded the swag. Once we left, they most likely called the police, who should be there by now. If either option one or three happened to Sals, we'll find out in a few days when the Inquirer is available."

Donnie looks at Maxo with a worried stare. "And if it's option two?"

Maxo sighs heavily as he pulls out a cigarette and sticks it in his mouth. "Then we're fucked."

Sure enough, the paper comes three days later. Smack-dab on the front page is a picture of Sals and Figs, dead on the edge of the river. Figs is belly up, with two shots on his front side, one in each lung and one shot under his chin. Sals is slumped over on his side, as if he fell over from a kneeling position, with one bullet hole in his temple.

The paper article reads as stated.

> Two firearms were retrieved at the scene of the murders, one of them found under the pants of a twenty-seven-year-old male identified as Juliano Paduli. The other firearm was found adjacent to the body of a forty-two-year-old male iden-

tified as Salvatore "Sals" Andresano, a known member of the Giambruno family run by Enzo Giambruno. This was without a doubt an organized hit planned by another family or perhaps the family itself. Only time will tell, as the police are searching both firearms for DNA and fingerprints. Hopefully, we will find out the person who committed this horrific act of violence.

Donnie is at home, just waking up from a restful night's sleep. He looks outside, the sun shining brightly through his bedroom window, bouncing off Kiara's angel-white nightgown. Rolling over, he kisses her on the cheek and gets out of bed. He walks out of the bedroom and into the kitchen, steaming up a hot pot of coffee.

After waiting a few minutes for the coffee to settle in the pot, he pours himself a cup and pours another for Kiara, walking her back to the bedroom and placing it on the bureau adjacent to the bed. He leaves the bedroom and opens the front door, his eyes meeting the front-page title, jumping off the screen in large bold lettering: "MURDER ON THE RIVER! TWO BODIES FOUND NEXT TO SCHUYLKILL IN PRESUMED MOB HIT!"

Donnie's face lights up with shock and a tinge of fear, but since he was inside the warehouse, he quickly brushes his paranoia away. He goes about his usual day as if nothing has changed. As Donnie's about to head out of the house, he hears a loud scream coming from the bathroom. He whips around quickly, grabbing a piece from a holster wrapped around his right ankle. He rushes up to the bathroom, the door closed, as he hears Kiara sobbing quietly. He backs away from the door and kicks it in, snapping the frame off the door and rushing into the bathroom, scaring Kiara in the process.

"What's happening? Are you okay? What the fuck happened?"

Kiara is on her knees, one hand covering her mouth, the other holding a piece of paper from the doctor's office.

"I'm okay, Donnie. I'm pretty fuckin' okay!"

Her tears aren't sad but joyous as she hands Donnie the paper, stating that the doctor has found pregnancy hormones in a urine sample taken at the doctors a few days prior. Donnie's hand combs his hair as tears of happiness roll down his cheek.

"We're gonna have a baby. We're gonna have a fuckin' baby. I'm gonna be a dad."

Donnie drops to his knees and lunges toward Kiara, kissing her and hugging her in their newly found parental happiness. Donnie and Kiara are going to be parents.

Sadly, this happiness doesn't last long. Donnie is out shopping for supplies to ready a room for the baby, which is still months away from being due but Donnie wants the kid to have the best house possible. While shopping, Donnie is approached by two boys in blue.

"Are you Donald McCullough?"

Donnie looks at the pair of officers, staring at them with his beany green eyes. "Depends on who's asking?"

"Philly PD's asking. We need you to come down to the station immediately."

Donnie looks back and forth between the two officers before sighing heavily. "Can I at least buy my shit first? I gotta kid on the way."

The officers look at each other before shaking their heads and escorting Donnie out of the store and into a cop car. The trip down to the station is like a one-way conversation talking to a wall. Donnie keeps asking questions, and the officers stay silent. Stuff like, "Can you at least tell me what I'm getting arrested for? I didn't do shit, why am I here? You guys are a bunch of fuckin' pigs." Shit like that.

After arriving at the station and being placed into an interrogation room, Donnie sits quietly for about ten minutes before one man walks into the room. He is dressed in black work pants, a light-blue long-sleeved, button-down collared shirt with a navy-blue tie and a badge hanging out of his left breast pocket. Donnie has one thought go through his head. This ain't no beat cop. This sure as fuck ain't no Philly PD.

As the man sits down, he places out a folder with a few papers inside of it on the table; and when he finally sits down, Donnie gets a clear read of his badge, stating in bolded blue letter, FEDERAL BUREAU OF INVESTIGATION, US SPECIAL AGENT.

Ah shit. After seeing his badge, Donnie slumps backward in his chair, showing no emotion but feeling a sprout of fear burrow itself in his stomach.

"Mr. McCullough, I am reaching out to you for help as you are in—pardon my French—a heap of shit right now."

The agent pulls out a newspaper and tosses it on the table, the same newspaper that shows on the front page both Sals's and Figs's bodies.

"What the fuck are you talking about? I don't fuckin' know these guys. Why the fuck am I here?"

The agent sighs lightly and pulls the paper away from Donnie, placing his hands on the table. "You do know these men, Mr. McCullough, as you killed them both."

Donnie's heart starts racing and pounding in his chest. "What the fuck are you talking about? I don't know these two people. They're fuckin' strangers to me. How the fuck did I kill them both when I've never even fuckin' met these guys?"

"Because, Mr. McCullough, your fingerprints were recovered on one of the firearms, the same firearm used to kill Mr. Paduli and Mr. Andresano. That is your heap of shit, Mr. McCullough."

Donnie's heart is racing even faster than before. His mind is having a conversation in his head, trying to figure out what happened. How the fuck did his fingerprints end up on Sals's gun? I never fuckin' touched his gun.

Until he did.

Donnie's face, if it wasn't emotionless before, is now after he came upon his sudden realization. Sals and Donnie swapped guns. Sals's .38 was acting up, and they swapped. Donnie never wiped it of prints. That's why it came up on only one gun. Donnie never touched Figs's piece. Without showing his fear, Donnie looks at the agent, smirking as he thinks.

"Okay. Say I did do it. I didn't do it 'cause I don't know these guys, but say I did whack these two fellas right here. How the fuck are you going to help me?"

"Well, Mr. McCullough, I know that you're an active member of the Giambruno family, working out of Mikey's Bar on East Girard.

I know you've been linked to at least three murders in Philadelphia, as well as having a checkered past, being arrested more than a few times."

Donnie restlessly looks at the agent and nods once.

"I know all about you, Mr. McCullough. I know that when you were ten, you went to your now late friend Jamey Giambruno's house after you saw your mother hold a gun to your father's head for you, your brother's, and your sister's protection. I know that you had to watch through the news your father walk out of your house in handcuffs and your mother in a body bag. I know because I was there, Mr. McCullough."

The agent pulls out a tattered business card and slides it across the table, the card reading through worn lettering, "Det. Jackson Freeman, Homicide. 555-3247."

A wave of shock covers Donnie's face as he slowly reaches his hand out and takes the business card.

"I've always wanted to help you, Donnie, and I still do."

After staring at the card for a few moments, he looks back up at Agent Freeman, seeing his familiar mustache, now a wintery-white color. He looks back and forth between the card and Agent Freeman. After a few quiet minutes, Donnie looks at Agent Freeman and sighs.

"What do I need to do?"

XXII

The Hard Truth

Donnie goes through his entire life of crime with Special Agent Freeman, unpacking the years he has longed to forget, all for it to become evidence against his best friends. As Donnie is talking to Agent Freeman, his mind flashes back to his first arrest where he stole and firebombed four cars under I-95, his mind narrowing down specifically to Sally Two's words before he stole the cars. Do whatever you want. Just don't get caught.

His mind then flashes to Sals who, other than Enzo, was practically a father to Donnie, talking to him before his court date. You never rat on your friends. Whether they did it or not is irrelevant. You never ever rat on your friends.

Donnie's mind is filled with uneasiness, his stomach churning in pain. Donnie would never do this. If Donnie was a different person watching a wise guy rat on his friends, he'd clip him himself. But Donnie has to do it. His mind jumps to the present moment to the thought of Kiara, the love of his life, newly married a month prior, now due with their first child in a few months. As much as his body and mind resists and hates him for doing it, Donnie continues to vomit information to Agent Freeman on everyone: Vinny Ruge, Maxo Salucci, Tino, Badger, Sally Two, even his own adoptive father, Enzo Giambruno.

Ratting out the only person who accepted you as a person, as someone who should be loved and not abused, takes its toll on Donnie. While telling Agent Freeman all of the details of a decade's worth of gangland activities, Donnie moves on to Enzo; and halfway through giving the agent information, Donnie begins crying, as if years and years of pain and anguish finally breaks through Donnie's stone-cold murderous heart.

Uninterrupted by the agent, Donnie cries long and hard, thinking back to the times where he and Ronan were first accepted into the Giambruno home; the time when the McCullough children are legally adopted by the Giambrunos; the many small jobs Enzo had Donnie run with his adoptive brother, Jamey, as well as the love and happiness he felt anytime Enzo was proud of Donnie while working with the guys.

All of that love, all of that pride, all of that happiness is now being thrown away for protection for his wife and future child. After Donnie's tears stop, he continues his criminal spiel. After spending six hours at the Philadelphia police department, Agent Freeman has enough evidence to send all of the guys away for a long time, essentially ending the reign of the Giambruno family in one fell swoop.

After finishing his interrogation, Agent Freeman packs up his notes and stands up to leave the room.

"You're free to go, Mr. McCullough."

Donnie nods somberly, his face covered with residual tears, standing up and making his way toward the door. Just as he exits, Donnie turns toward Agent Freeman with a curious tone in his voice. "How exactly will the WPP help me and my family?

While not divulging details yet, Agent Freeman offers his reassurances. "Don't worry about it, Mr. McCullough. I will take care of everything. I promise."

Donnie nods and exits the room just as Agent Freeman shouts out the open doorway. "I'd tell your wife though."

Donnie's face grimaces as the Agent yells his explanation. Fuck. I figured he'd say that.

Donnie heads home to Kiara, who is used to him coming home at two in the morning from his "bar job," now walking through the door at nine thirty in the evening.

"You're home from work early."

Donnie sighs quietly before walking up to Kiara with a dejected look covering his face.

"'Cause I wasn't at work, Kay."

Confused now, Kiara turns to look at Donnie with a curious peer. "Why weren't you at work?"

Donnie sighs as he walks over to the couch with Kiara coming to sit next to him.

"We gotta talk. There's something I need to tell you about."

After Kiara sits down, Donnie lays it all on her. How he had been working as an associate for the Giambruno family since he was thirteen years old, how he had grown up in a life of crime and continued it through his wise guy lifestyle, even hinting at saying he had done hits for the family without going into the nitty-gritty details. After explaining his life of crime, he continues to explain that he wasn't at work, about how the FBI is willing to help Donnie and Kiara through the witness protection program, how Donnie can leave his life of crime and live a full life with Kiara and their future child.

After spending around twenty minutes talking, Donnie stops and looks at Kiara, whose face is emotionless. No shock. No tears. No anger. Nothing. Kiara just looks at Donnie, processing everything he had just told her, hoping it was all a dream or a joke or anything but reality. Absolute silence covers the room like the quiet darkness covers the sky after a sunset. After a few minutes, Kiara stands up and looks at Donnie as a single tear sprouts and rolls quickly down her cheek. "Is it true?"

Hiding his face, Donnie stares at the ground and nods his head. He raises his head after a few moments and is met with a firm slap across the face from Kiara. After slapping her husband, Kiara retreats to the bedroom, the door slam echoing through the apartment, followed by loud audible cries. Donnie doesn't chase Kiara. Donnie doesn't even move.

After her slap, Donnie covers his face in shame and cries. After revealing the truth of his past and of his lifestyle within the mob, Donnie knows Kiara is done with him. He knows that when come tomorrow, she'll leave Donnie, taking their child with her. These thoughts flood and overwhelm Donnie's mind as he lays his head down on the living room couch, slowly crying himself to sleep.

The next morning, Donnie wakes up and looks around the room, listening intently for anything. A footstep, a click, a sound. After hearing nothing for a few minutes, his face furrows with depression as he gets up off the couch and walks toward the bedroom, reaching for the handle. To his surprise, it's unlocked, and he turns it, peeking into the bedroom.

He sees Kiara, sleeping soundly on the bed, her backside facing Donnie. His heart calms down and he sighs happily, quietly shutting the door and going to make coffee. After pouring himself a cup, he pours one for Kiara and walks it into the bedroom, leaving it on her nightstand. He exits and sits down on the couch, sipping his coffee, waiting for Kiara to wake up.

After a few minutes, Donnie hears footsteps from inside the bedroom. His heart begins racing a little bit and picks up as the bedroom door opens, revealing Kiara, clutching her mug of coffee, dressed in a bathrobe, her pregnant stomach creating a small hump under the robe. She peers at Donnie, who smiles slightly before it disappears from embarrassment.

"Morning, Kay."

After taking a few sips, Kiara hobbles over to Donnie, who stands up to look at her. The couple lock eyes, Kiara staring at Donnie intently, forming a question in her head. "How can this witness protection program help us?"

As Kiara says this, Donnie sighs happily and starts laughing nervously, drawing a curious look from his wife.

"What's so funny?"

"I thought that you were gonna say that you wanted to divorce me."

Kiara sighs and nods at Donnie, taking a few more sips of her coffee. "I was, Donnie. After last night, I was so angry, sad, upset, disappointed. I was everything. That's why I hit you. 'Cause I knew if I didn't, I was going to say something that I'd regret. I thought long and hard about you, Donnie. About us. All three of us."

Kiara looks down and places one hand on her stomach, caressing it gently. "And I knew that if I left you, our child would be fatherless, and I would be husbandless."

Donnie nods a few times and looks at Kiara, who is staring at her stomach in motherly love.

"I'm all done now, Kay. I'm done with the mob. I'm done for good. I want to be a father now."

Kiara looks at Donnie as her lips purse to a slight smile.

"And a husband."

Donnie watches as her smile grows slightly with every second she looks at him.

"I love you, Kay. Both of you."

Donnie gets down on his knee and kisses his wife's stomach, as Kiara's smile grows ever bigger. Donnie stands up and looks at Kiara, smiling happily before kissing her.

"We'll get through this, Kay. I promise you. We will get through this."

Kiara nods happily as the couple hug each other, standing in the living room in a fleeting moment of loving embrace.

XXIII

Screaming for Life

The sounds of ripping Velcro and metallic clicks echo through one of the many SWAT warehouses in Philadelphia. Inside the warehouse contains twenty-some law enforcement officers, varying from Philly PD to SWAT to FBI.

Special Agent Freeman and his team of four are leading this SWAT raid on Mikey's bar in an attempt to bring down the Giambruno crime family. The team slaps on their bulletproof vests and holsters their service revolvers. After around an hour of checking, double-checking, and triple checking their gear, Agent Freeman gathers the officers into a small circle to explain their plan.

"All right, gentlemen. We got a job to do today." Agent Freeman walks over to a large cork board with various pictures of members of the Giambruno family organization. There is Enzo Giambruno, with the word Boss scribbled next to him. Massimo Salucci, Tito Valentino, Salvatore Andresano and Vincenzo Ruggerio, all written as underbosses with a tag taped across Salvatore Andresano's picture that read DECEASED in big, bold letters. There were pictures of all of the wise guys in a line across the board, like pawns protecting their king, only this game was life.

The pictures consist of Mickey Callaghan, Nicolo Russo, Benito Balboni, Salvatore Banetti, and Donnie's picture, lined up in a line completing the base of the criminal pyramid. Of course, all pictures had names and nicknames under all the pictures. Off to the side of the pyramid is a picture of Shane O'Brien and Juliano Paduli, both with DECEASED tags draped across their pictures. Mickey and Nicolo's pictures, instead of deceased tags, had tags with large black question marks placed over their two photos.

"We are raiding Mikey's Bar, the suspected headquarters of the Giambruno family. We are looking for these individuals." Agent Freeman lifts a long meter stick and taps on all the pictures not labelled DECEASED or "?."

"Most nights, they are all there, either drinking at the bar or downstairs in the basement. We suspect that the basement is where they run their meetings, possibly even their gambling ring. The basement does not have any exits, so anyone running will have to make it through the backdoor exit or the front door. Me and my people will lead inside with an additional five officers, five will take the back alleyway door, and five will remain on the street in case any make it past us. We're hitting the place tonight at nine thirty."

Agent Freeman turns his wrist and peers at his watch. "About that time now, gentlemen. Lock and load. Vans out in five!"

A flurry of nods and approving grunts ripple through the crowd as Agent Freeman checks his gun once more before loading into a modified tractor trailer to act as disguise as they approach the bar. Inside the trailer are about forty seats, all mounted to the side of the truck with bags of ammo, weapons, body armor, and more sitting in the back corner of the truck.

A few minutes pass, and the entire warehouse is inside of the trailer, the door shut tight and en route to Mikey's Bar on East Girard. The ride remains silent, the rattle of metal after hitting a bump becoming the only sound being heard inside the trailer. After about ten minutes, two knocks from the driver's area echo through the trailer, signaling their arrival at the location. A SWAT officer opens the door, and a way of blue empties onto the nighttime sidewalks of Fishtown. Since the truck is parked next to the alleyway, ten officers head in that direction, and ten head toward the front. Agent Freeman, before entering the bar, takes one long deep breath, as if it might be his last.

In a fragment of speed and energy, Agent Freeman and the officers burst into the bar, quickly spreading through the room. The barflies in the upper room jump in surprise from the team of officers with guns drawn rush through the front door of their neighborhood bar. A man, quickly identified by Agent Freeman as Tito "Tino" Valentino, stares at the door as they enter and, in a flash, shoots downstairs to the lower bar room. Tino looks at the overly packed basement of Mikey's Bar and shouts at the crowd in his thick Sicilian accent.

"BLUE! BLUE!"

Like a coop of scared chickens, the basement crowd scatters toward the steps, bull-rushing the officers upstairs. The first ones hitting the upper-level room get snagged by the officers, but due to the immense number of people rushing the agents, crowds evade the police presence inside the bar before running right into the arms of the backup SWAT members guarding the office.

Even then, a few make it past the labyrinth of officers surrounding the bar sidewalk, the majority being caught and dragged away to the tractor trailer, now acting as a makeshift paddy wagon for the arrested. As the police officers round up the remaining patrons, Agent Freeman and his team head toward the basement, clearing room after room, all empty before entering Enzo's office, where he and Maxo Salucci are sitting peacefully, smoking cigars and drinking whiskey. Though he's initially caught off guard by the eerie stillness of the pair, Agent Freeman holsters his service revolver as the rest of the team enters the office room.

"Enzo Giambruno, Massimo Salucci, you're under arrest."

Enzo's face remains emotionless as he takes a few long puffs of his cigar, staring at the agents with a look that could melt ice. "Under what grounds, Agent?"

Agent Freeman spits out a laundry list of charges at Enzo, who listens respectfully to the agent. After finishing, Enzo nods at Maxo, who stands up and places his wrists behind his back, one of the agents handcuffing the captain before leaving his office. After Maxo is escorted to the trailer, only Enzo and Agent Freeman remain in the now silent basement office of Mikey's Bar. Enzo finishes his whiskey glass and walks to Agent Freeman, coming within inches of his face, the smell of whiskey from Enzo's lips bouncing off Agent Freeman's silver mustache.

"You...don't...have...shit."

Enzo smirks and turns around, calmly placing his wrist behind his back. Agent Freeman unhooks his handcuffs from his belt and slaps them on his wrists, latching them more tightly than usual, causing Enzo to wince slightly from the slam of the cuffs.

"I wouldn't be so sure about that."

After the trailer makes it back at the station, now overflowing with petrified barflies and mobsters, Enzo sits in an interrogation room, cuffed to the table, surrounded by officers, waiting patiently and quietly, feeling the eyes of the officers stare a hole through him.

"Can I at least get my phone call? Let the wife know I won't be home tonight?"

Enzo's remark is followed by a horrifying chuckle, ripping through the silent air like a sickle through wheat, causing the officers to slightly recoil. Luckily, moments later, Agent Freeman walks through the door, with a combination of fear and resolve stretched across his aged face. He slaps a folder down and slides a metal fold-up chair to the table, slowly flipping through file and file as Enzo stares at him questionably. After a few minutes of quiet scanning, Agent Freeman sighs heavily and closes the folder, leaning back in his chair and inspecting Enzo's facial structure and body language for a few moments.

"I'm gonna be honest with you Enzo, you—"

"That's Mr. Giambruno to you, fuckface!"

Enzo's face erupts with an indignant look as aversion quickly spreads across Agent Freeman's face before he politely corrects himself.

"I'm gonna be honest with you, Mr. Giambruno. You are going to jail until you die."

His anger quickly turned to laughter, his thick voice ripping through the air before stopping a few seconds later.

"The fuck I am! You don't have shit on me."

Agent Freeman purses his lips and nods slowly. The agent's hand slowly hovers to the file; and he lifts it up slowly, his eyes meeting the label, reading Enzo Giambruno. He turns it the mafia boss' way and slides it into his hand.

Enzo looks at the file with his name on it, staring at it before chuckling heartily, grabbing the file a few seconds later.

"I'll humor you, Agent."

He opens the folder, and there are no files at all. No photographs. No police records. No birth records. No nothing except about five loose-leaf papers full from top to bottom, covered in handwritten notes by Agent Freeman with details from a decade's worth of mafia activities: robberies, gambling, prostitution, shylocking deals, beatings, murders, all described firsthand by Enzo's adoptive son and Giambruno family associate, Donnie McCullough, though Enzo doesn't know it.

As he reads the notes, top to bottom, front and back, Enzo's face goes through a roller coaster of emotions: from confusion, pain, anger, and sadness to joy, laughter, and happiness. In the end, Enzo closes the file and sighs loudly, his heavy Sicilian figure sinking into the table and his head into his hands. Agent Freeman motions to the two officers, who stood as protection for Agent Freeman if Enzo broke free, to leave the room.

After leaving, Agent Freeman leans back in his chair, staring at Enzo's face, remaining motionless in his hands. After a few minutes of still silence, Enzo breaks down in loud, audible cries, letting out years and years' worth of pain in an interrogation room in downtown Philadelphia where, after reading those five pages of notes, Enzo will be gone for good. He doesn't even try to dispute it. He knows it's all true. He accepts it for what it is.

After a few minutes, Agent Freeman grabs the folder and stands up, walking over to Enzo, whispering into his ear while he is still crying. "I'll see you in court, Enzo."

As he begins to walk out of the room, Enzo cuts off the agent's timely exit. "Wait! Can you at least tell me who talked?"

"I'm sorry, Mr. Giambruno. Witness confidentiality."

Enzo's face breaks out with tears again, this time with a shade of anger rushing over his face.

"You fuckin' pigs and your legal bullshit. That's what you are. Fuckin' pigs. All of ya!"

Agent Freeman snaps and steams toward Enzo, looking to beat him right there. The agent brings his nose within inches of Enzo's face before saying the words, "That's Special Agent Freeman to you, fuckface!"

After that, Agent Freeman leaves the room, Enzo shouting at him through the open door. "I don't care where I am. slammer or not, I'll find your witness and I'll kill that fuckin' bastard! You hear me? I'll kill him!"

An officer slams the door to the interrogation, Enzo still screaming behind the closed steel door, knowing that is how he will spend the rest of his life.

XXIV

US v. Enzo GIAMBRUNO Et Al.

Donnie is sitting in a hotel room about twenty minutes away from the courthouse where, as of right now, all of his friends and fellow wise guys are being tried for everything that Agent Freeman was told about on that piece of paper; and without a doubt, all of them are pleading the fifth, even though they know they did it.

That's where Donnie comes in. Even if they all plead innocent, Donnie is their Hail Mary. In Donnie's mind, he's everything that the guys do before a job. He's the last drag of a cigarette, the final sip of whiskey, that quick kiss on your wife or your girlfriend—all the things you do one more time before heading out, knowing that you might not come back. Donnie is the final thing.

He puts on a new suit, one that he stole during the warehouse raid that left Sal and Figs dead. His court outfit is a light beige color with a diamond-encrusted watch on his left wrist and various golden rings on each hand, and with black Oxford shoes freshly shined and glasses-tinted black. He looks at his watch, reading 10:00 a.m. sharp. He wets his hair and slicks back his hair before leaving the hotel room. A police officer standing watch outside of the room escorts Donnie down to the lobby and out of the hotel where a police car is standing by, waiting for him to take him to become the final nail in the coffin of the Giambruno crime family.

Meanwhile, the Senate congressional subcommittee is sitting in Joseph A. Burns Courthouse in Philadelphia with Senator Willem V Rothman Jr., aided by the committee chairman Samuel Nells, leading the investigation. Moments later, Senator Willem Rothman watches as Enzo Giambruno and his fourteen associates enter the court-room, the associates ranging from low-level button men to high-level caporegimes. The Senate committee converse amongst themselves quietly as news cameras flash brightly, over and over like a relentless lightness storm, taking picture after picture of the Giambruno crime family.

"Please remain standing for the sworn testimony."

Just about to sit but interrupted by the senator, Enzo and his associates all stand up and prepare for the start of the case.

"Raise your right hand."

Almost in unison, fifteen hands shoot up to semiright angle gestures as the senator reads aloud to the crowd.

"Do you solemnly swear that you will tell the truth, the whole truth, and nothing but the truth, so help you God?"

Various responses erupt from the fifteen men, ranging from the typical "I do" to "I will" to "Sure, whatever." After swearing in, the men all sit down, almost all of them except for a few button men having their own different lawyers.

"Please state your name and where you reside, please."

Murmurous conversation erupts between the lawyers and their clients, the men talking for a few brief seconds before they make their statements.

"Under advice from my counsel, I am invoking my Fifth Amendment right under the United States Constitution in order to not incriminate myself."

Though he saw this coming, Senator Rothman sighs heavily as one by one, each associate of the Giambruno family, including Enzo, plead their Fifth Amendment rights, refusing to speak to the subcommittee about any allegations of criminal activity. For the next half hour, Senator Rothman and Chairman Nells ask question after question to various members of the Giambruno family as they take the witness stand, all of them being closed with their legal employment of the Fifth Amendment.

If not for Donnie, this case would have been for naught. At ten thirty, almost on the dot, a crowd of police enter the courtroom, escorting their only hope of a case, Donnie McCullough. Shielding his eyes from the stares of his friends and father, Donnie's tinted black shades reflect the horrified and distraught looks of his family, the only family that he cared about, the family that raised him and showed him love ever since he became an orphaned child in 1959.

In the rows and rows of newspeople in the courtroom, he spots Stella, his adoptive mother, dressed in a white dress, sniffling and covering her eyes with a matching white handkerchief. Donnie becomes overwhelmed with regret and his eyes well up with tears, but he wipes them away before they roll down below his glasses.

"Mr. McCullough, please enter the witness stand."

Senator Rothman's voice cut into Donnie's sadness, and Donnie regained his composure. He nods silently as he walks up to the witness stand. The court bailiff, a stocky, thirty-year-old white man, swears Donnie into court. After saying those dreaded two words no wise guy should ever say and mean, Donnie sits down at the witness stand.

"Mr. McCullough, please state your name and current residence."

"Donald Aingeal McCullough, 439 Redins Street, South Philadelphia."

Senator Rothman nods happily, as this is the first time he hasn't heard a Fifth Amendment plea today.

"Mr. McCullough, do you acknowledge that by agreeing to appear before this committee, you agree to disclose any information regarding the Giambruno family in exchange for your immunity despite your involvement in some of these activities?"

"I do."

Those two words take the wind out of Donnie. His body becomes heavy, his legs become weak, and his mind becomes a blur. Luckily, he is able to reach for a bottle of water that's sitting on the witness desk. After taking a few sips, his body recuperates and his spiel begins.

The trail goes from a half-hour flop of a RICO case to being three hours' worth of evidence, explaining everything he had seen, heard, been told to do, or has done over a decade-long span: witness executions in broad daylight, the mysterious disappearances of Frankie Garcetti and Jimmy Barseni, the alcohol-induced murder of Joey Slur, various rackets involving the basement gambling ring, and Books's many point-shaving schemes, as well as shylocking and doing swag runs out of the Schuylkill River warehouse, where Sals's and Figs's bodies were discovered.

The committee takes a short recess for lunch at around noon. When they resume court about a half hour later, Donnie is only about halfway done. He continues until around two in the afternoon when Donnie finally finishes. Once he stops, Donnie takes a look at Enzo for the first time since he entered the stand, his view panning over to Stella and then all of his brothers-in-arms—from Maxo, Tino, and Vinny Ruge to Sally Two and Badger—all staring at Donnie, devastated by Donnie's words. Some showing pain, others showing anger, but all showing their disappointment in Donnie.

He had let them down in the worst possible way by turning on them.

He holds himself until he leaves the courtroom and gets back to the hotel room, escorted by Agent Freeman.

Almost immediately after getting through the door, Donnie grabs a bottle of whiskey from his bag and takes a long swig straight from the bottle, remnants of the liquid flowing over his lips and onto his impressive suit. Agent Freeman waits patiently at the doorway, watching Donnie's "method" of calming himself before walking up to him, calmly placing a hand on his shoulder.

"You did good today, Donnie."

Like the drop of a dime, Donnie snaps, slamming the bottle on the table and turning around quickly, grabbing the aged agent by his shirt collar, trying to lift him up but to no avail due to his height and weight.

"You promise me my family will be safe!"

Agent Freeman looks at Donnie, whose face is now covered in tears, falling uncontrollably down his cheeks.

"You fuckin' promise that once this case is over, I'm long gone, far away from this godforsaken city, far away from any danger that could harm my family. Because I just turned my back on the people who cared for me. I've seen what they've done to witnesses because I've done the jobs myself. Promise me, Agent Freeman. Please."

Donnie breaks down, his grieving face meeting the agent's chest as the desolation of his situation overwhelms him. Agent Freeman doesn't fight Donnie, nor does he push him away. He lets Donnie let it out, all of his pain of the case and all of the thoughts of how Enzo and Stella looked at him up on the witness stand, betraying the family that raised him. After a few minutes, Agent Freeman gently pulls Donnie away from him, making his eyes meet Donnie's. "I promise."

The subcommittee calls for recess, beginning again a week later. In that week, a grand jury will decide whether Donnie's three-hour long witness testimony worked or not. Regardless of the outcome, Donnie would be heading off to wherever the WPP sent him, Kiara, and their baby. If the Giambruno family is indicted, Donnie's chances of being whacked are essentially nonexistent, as many of Enzo's soldiers will be given hefty sentences for major felonies such as murder and armed robbery. If not indicted, Donnie's chances of being made, wherever he may be, while still low, will never be zero.

The week after, the case comes and goes. The day of arraignment is awaiting the Giambruno family. As all fifteen members enter the court, Donnie sits in the back of the courtroom, joined by Agent Freeman, awaiting the decision of the jury. At around 11:15 a.m., the jury enters the room, taking their spots at the jury box as the foreperson steps forward, standing before the judge, the lawyers, and fifteen of the most dangerous men in Philadelphia.

"Have you and the jury reached a verdict?"

"We have, Your Honor."

The entirety of the courtroom comes to a standstill as the leading juror reads the statement from the page.

"On twenty-four counts murder in the first degree, twenty-two counts of murder in the second degree, forty counts conspiracy to commit murder, fourteen counts of armed robbery, sixty counts of illegal gambling, thirty counts of illegal prostitution, twelve counts of illegal loansharking, thirty-three counts of assault and battery, forty-five counts of usage of unregistered firearms with intent to commit murder, fifty counts of possession of unregistered firearms, seventeen counts of theft and twenty-eight counts of grand larceny, we find all defendants guilty."

Donnie's hand covers his face as tears slowly roll down his cheeks. The courtroom lights up like the sun as camera flashes cut through the air, taking picture after picture of the police officers placing cuffs of the Giambruno family and escorting them from the courtroom, one by one. Agent Freeman turns to Donnie and shakes his hand firmly.

"You did it, Donnie. Congratulations."

Despite his feelings of regret, Donnie is happy that he untimely chose a good future for his child instead of the road that he went down as a child. Donnie waits in the courtroom until empty, reveling in its once booming nature not too long ago. Donnie sits in the courtroom that in his head feels like an eternity before Agent Freeman's voice reels him back to reality.

"Time to go, Donnie."

With that, Donnie gets up and leaves the courtroom, heading to the car that is escorting him back to the hotel. Just as he is about to get into the car, Agent Freeman extends his hand to Donnie who firmly shakes it as the agent whispers the only words that would calm Donnie's nerves.

"I promise."

Epilogue

Ronan stares intently at the blackboard, jotting down note after note from his college mathematics class. His professor, a tall, lanky man with a white hairstyle in a ponytail that went down past his shoulder blades, scratches away at the board, writing equations for the class to complete. After a few minutes, the bell rings; and the class, once silent, is now bustling with closing notebooks, papers being shoved into bags, and footsteps exiting the classroom.

"Be sure to write down these equations and finish them as homework."

Ronan picks up his writing pace, turning his neat handwriting into lazily written chicken scratch, finishing his notes a few seconds later before leaving the classroom, heading home for the weekend.

Ronan is a nineteen-year-old college student at New Hampshire University, freshly entering his sophomore year. He commutes to and from school from his home in the small city of Durham. His father, Carson Mitchell, is a union man working for the United Brotherhood of Carpenters. Carson has lived in New Hampshire since he was born. After spending a few years in the union, Carson married his high school sweetheart, Katrina Murphy, in 1972. About a year later, in 1973, is when the Mitchell family had their one and only child, Ronan Donald Mitchell.

After getting home, Ronan sees his father mowing the lawn shirtless, showing off his impressively built body for a forty-year-old man. Ronan peers through the kitchen window, seeing his mother doing the dishes and preparing to make dinner.

"Hey, Pops."

"Hey, Ro. How was school?"

"Ah, it's a bunch of bullshit, Dad. I don't understand half of whatever he's talking about. After a few minutes, everything sounds the same."

"Hey, I know how you feel. I felt that way in high school. I'm happy I was able to graduate and get the hell outta there. Why don't I bring you to work one day, let you see what your old man does all day. See if you like it or not."

Ronan looks at his father, whose rugged face scrunches, as if he's hiding something important; but Ronan brushes it off.

"Ronan!"

Ronan whips around to face his mother, whose head is sticking out of the kitchen window.

"Could you help me for a minute please?"

"Yeah, Ma. Be there in a sec."

Ronan turns back to his dad, who has just finished the lawn and is now rolling the mower back to the garage.

"We'll talk later about math. See if we can get you some help at school. I promise."

"All right, Dad."

"Now go help your mother."

Ronan nods and walks inside to aid his mother in her needs. After rolling it back into the garage, Carson takes a swig of ice water from a cup sitting on a table. Hanging above the table is a calendar, dated the current year of 1992. He looks at what day it is and sighs, his mind quickly fading away. Almost twenty years now. His eyes move from the calendar to a newspaper article, a few years old, with the front page shouting in its bold font, "PHILLY MOB BOSS DIES IN PRISON."

He glances at the page, reading a few brief sentences before turning away and walking inside the house. He takes a quick shower to clean himself of the sweat and grass that flooded his pores less than ten minutes ago. After getting out, he dresses himself in a semi-nice outfit of khakis, a yellow polo shirt, and a leather bomber jacket as his wife enters the bedroom.

"Where are you off to?"

"St. Jude's. I need to clear my head. I think I'm gonna talk to someone today."

Katrina's eyes light up with happiness as she wraps her arms around her husband.

"I'm happy for you, Carson. This'll be good for you."

"I know it will. I know."

Carson pulls himself away and quickly pecks his wife on the lips. "I'll be home soon, Kat. I love you."

"Love you too, Carson."

He hops in the car and pulls out of the driveway, heading out on his way to the neighborhood church of St. Jude's Church. After parking, he walks into the church, completely empty, with the exception of a priest setting up for daily mass.

"Hey, Father."

"Good afternoon, sir."

"I know you're busy, Father, but I was wondering if we could talk."

The priest sets down a folded-up altar cover on the table.

"Is this a one-on-one kind of talk or a confession kind of talk?"

Carson looks at the priest and nods slowly. "Confession kind of talk, Father."

The priest nods and walks over to the confessional, sitting down in the priest's booth, with Carson sitting in the penitent's booth. Carson kneels down and silently performs the sign of the cross.

"Bless me, Father, for I have sinned. It has been…three weeks since my last confession."

The priest calmly grunts in approval as Carson's face enters his opened hands.

"Where do I start, Father? I haven't been completely honest with you every time I've come to see you, Father."

"It's okay, my son. You can tell me."

Reluctantly but happily, Carson unravels his life before the priest.

"I've done things, Father. Terrible things. Horrible things. I've robbed, cheated, stolen from people in exorbitant amounts and from those who needed it more. I've beaten people within inches of their lives. I've tortured people for money, for greed, for power. I've even gone as far as to commit murder, Father. I'm a horrible person, Father."

At this point, Carson's face is now welling with tears, the sounds of loud sniffles echoing through the barren church.

"I don't deserve this, Father. I don't deserve to be forgiven, Father. I deserve to die myself, Father."

"No, no, no, no. You don't, my son. You do deserve forgiveness. You do deserve God's love. You say that you've done these…things without remorse. Yet here you are, confessing to me through painful, tearful, remorseful sorrow and regret. You deserve forgiveness."

Carson lets a sigh of pain as he continues to cry into his hand, shielding his face from the priest in bitter shame.

"It's okay. It takes a lot of guts to admit the wrongs you've done. It takes a lot of remorse to admit the things you've done. As long as you show that remorse and admit to God that you have indeed done wrong, you will always be forgiven."

Carson sniffles loudly. His tears stop, and his head lifts from his hands.

"For your penance, I want you to a rosary, dedicating it to Mary."

"Okay, Father."

"Now, say your act of contrition."

In the final few minutes, Carson recites the penitential prayer as the priest intently listens to the words. Upon completion, the priest silently mumbles a few words of absolution before saying aloud, "I absolve you of these and all your sins, in the name of the Father, and of the Son, and of the Holy Spirit. Amen."

"Thank you, Father. Have a good day."

While feeling a weight lift from his shoulders, before Carson can fully stand, the same weight hits him in the chest. Carson loses his breath momentarily and stumbles backward, his body resting against the back of the confessional. He looks up to see a small hole in the divider between the priest and Carson. He looks at the hole and then at his chest, as a small blotch of blood calmly begins to grow on his yellow polo shirt. Quickly turning white, he turns to look at the divider, where he can see the priest, standing to his feet, clutching a suppressed pistol in his hand.

"Say hi to Enzo for me."

His mind goes black and his body goes limp as a quick shot from the pistol smacks Donnie square in the forehead. Blood begins to cascade down his face like a river of death as the priest makes his way out of the church. Just before leaving, he turns to face the altar, with a marble-sculpted crucifix hanging over it. He peers at the floor to the left, seeing a blood pool on the floor, slowly growing bigger. After a moment. He faces the statue of Jesus Christ, his face emotionless, and bows his head in respect.

About the Author

Daniel Montvydas is a two-time self-published author and is currently enlisted in the United States military as a US Marine. He has been writing since sophomore year of high school, inspired by his teachers, parents, family and friends, as well as my many extracurricular activities, past, present, and future.

CPSIA information can be obtained
at www.ICGtesting.com
Printed in the USA
LVHW041253190323
741950LV00002B/197